Mary Ann walked into Greg's bar and spotted the firefighters right away. Trey had his back to the door and Theresa was bent over him practically shoving her cleavage in his face. Nope, this was not happening. That was her hotshot, and she wasn't sharing, thank you very much. Guess it was time to stake her claim.

Mary Ann walked over and cooed, "Trey darling, there you are, sorry I was late." She pushed between Theresa and her man, grabbed his face and kissed him like there was no tomorrow. At first, he was a little hesitant, probably from shock at her forwardness, but after just a few seconds he got right on board and kissed her back with passion.

The kiss was so hot and delicious that she almost didn't hear Theresa say, "How rude," and flounce off.

Trey kissed her another minute or two, then pulled back and grinned. "Thanks for saving me."

"Not saving you so much as staking a claim, but you're welcome."

"Staking a claim? I think I like that. Would you like to stake your claim out on the dance floor?"

"Yes, I would." She dropped her purse on the table where the rest of the firefighters were sitting in open mouthed astonishment at her audacity. She looked at them, shrugged and said, "You snooze, you lose."

They burst out laughing and Trey pulled her out on the floor. He drew her close and she could feel his strong muscular body fitting very well with her softer one. The song was a fast ballad; the perfect 'get to know you better' dance with a handsome man. Trey was handsome, and he smelled good too, like outdoors, fresh air, and man, with a very faint hint of aftershave and wood smoke. Trey held her close and twirled her around the dance floor. He felt so darn good against her that she'd have been happy to stay like this for a week, maybe two.

FIRE ON THE MOUNTAIN

A LAKE CHELAN NOVEL

SHIRLEY PENICK

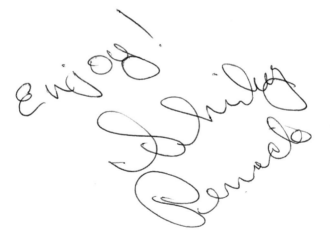

FIRE ON THE MOUNTAIN

Photography by Jean Woodfin
Cover models: Kim and Tony Hadeed
Cover design by Shirley Smuda Media
Editing by Carol Tietsworth
Formatting by Cora Cade

Contact me:
www.shirleypenick.com
www.facebook.com/ShirleyPenickAuthor
To sign up for Shirley's New Release Newsletter, send email to
shirleypenick@outlook.com, subject newsletter.

To the first responders
who put their lives on the line
every single day to save ours.
Thank you for your dedication and service.

To the people who have had a wildfire
bearing down on them, I hope you did not
suffer loss from it, and if you did may
God bless and keep you.

ALSO BY SHIRLEY PENICK

LAKE CHELAN SERIES

The Rancher's Lady: A Lake Chelan novella

Hank and Ellen's story

Sawdust and Satin: Lake Chelan #1

Chris and Barbara's story

Designs on Her: Lake Chelan #2

Nolan and Kristen's story

Smokin': Lake Chelan #3

Jeremy and Amber's story

Fire on the Mountain: Lake Chelan #4

Trey and Mary Ann's story

BURLAP AND BARBED WIRE SERIES

A Cowboy for Alyssa: Burlap and Barbed Wire #1

Beau and Alyssa's story

Taming Adam: Burlap and Barbed Wire #2

Adam and Rachel's story

Coming Soon! Tempting Chase: Burlap and Barbed Wire #3

Chase and Katie's story

CHAPTER 1

$\mathcal{T}$rey Peterson trudged up the hill with the rest of his hotshot crew. He was so damn glad they had finally gotten all of the hotspots out, in what used to be a meadow, and were heading over the hill to the next area. Team Alpha was to the southeast and Team Charlie was to the northwest. Their team, Bravo, was in the middle, moving toward Charlie to join forces.

"Looks like it's worse up ahead than what we just finished," one of the rookies said.

Kevin the Crew Boss nodded. "That's what we're here for, kid. We're headed toward a more forested area where the heavy fuel is, we were just taking it easy in the valley. Now we're going to put in some real work."

Team Alpha would either join them when they had their area contained or continue eastward, depending on what was needed. They had been deployed into the field for three days by this point and had no idea when they would be returning to base. These fires in the Chelan Valley in eastern Washington state had started out small and very remote.

The first responders had been a fire jumper crew and one

helicopter. Since the location was so remote and in such a rugged wilderness area, everyone thought the smoke jumper crew would be able to handle the problem. But then the wind had shifted, and dry lightning had started other fires that merged with what was already burning.

It had since grown into a huge fire storm that was moving rapidly toward the town, and the residents that lived on the mountains above the small town of Chedwick, Washington. That's when they had called in a second helicopter and the hotshot crews. Their crew, the Fighting Jaguars, were working from the Chedwick side of the fire and another two crews were working from the Lucerne side, to create fire breaks between the inferno raging on the mountain and the towns.

They finally reached the top of the hill and could see the work that lay ahead. Yeah it was going to be a hell of a lot of work and a long time before they got a day off, fire was everywhere and there was plenty of fuel.

Trey glanced back the way they had come. "Dammit, look." He pointed down into the valley and they all turned to look.

"Well fuck, a flare up. But we've got a shit storm ahead of us." Kevin shook his head.

Trey spoke up, "Kevin, I'm quick, I'll head back and put out that little trouble-maker and be back with you before Quinn gets the first tree felled."

Kevin nodded. "Not the best solution. I don't like us to be separated, but I can't see taking the whole team back for that. We can't leave it either, that valley leads to some homes, which is why we were there to begin with, rather than in the forest. Alright, Trey, head back but keep in touch."

"Yes sir." Trey saluted and turned around to hustle back to the far side of the valley to put out the flare up.

As he charged back into the valley he thought about how

lucky they were on this fire. Base was normally just a camp when fighting wild land fires, but one of the residents that lived on the mountain had offered her house for their use when she had to be evacuated. After what was probably a boatload of paperwork the Fighting Jaguars had taken her up on the offer.

Crossing a small stream bed, Trey thought back to that day a few weeks ago, going in to help evacuate the woman and finding all those acetylene tanks just waiting to blow them to hell and gone. But even more incendiary than the gas, was the cute little brunette, Mary Ann, who had been helping her friend evacuate. The Fighting Jaguars had been getting ready to deploy out into the firestorm when Kevin called out to him.

"Trey, get over to that house on the ridge and find out why the hell they haven't evacuated. Do they not see the forty-foot flames?"

"Yes, sir." Trey saluted his crew boss as he hot footed it out of the forest and across the road. The wind had grown in the night and now the whole damn mountain was on fire. He hustled into the yard and saw a woman pulling the cop, who had probably come to evacuate her, toward a shed.

He ran up to the pair. "We've got to get this place evacuated now."

"Oh two, hallelujah!" The woman grabbed hold of his arm and started dragging them both towards the shed.

Trey asked, "Ma'am, just what's in the shed that's so important to risk your life?"

"The tanks," she said.

The cop shook his head. "But you told me they were loaded."

"The household tanks, yes," she shoved both of them through the door to the shed, "but not these."

"Oh shit," the men spoke in unison. There, standing next to the door, were over a half dozen four-foot acetylene tanks. Trey called

for assistance and they got the tanks loaded into the truck just as some men from town came to help.

Once the tanks were loaded he went over to urge the woman's friend to evacuate. She was a knockout, even all disheveled and dirty from loading up the truck and trying to move the tanks. "I'm Trey, it's not safe for a pretty lady like you to be on this mountain."

"I know, but I couldn't just leave my friend up here to fend for herself. I'm Mary Ann."

"Mary Ann, that's very loyal, but now that she's got help, you should head down to safety. We don't want anything to happen to you."

Mary Ann blushed. "I'll get going. Look me up if you get a break. Mary Ann Thompson."

"Will do, I'll buy you a beer or glass of wine or whatever, as thanks for not leaving us to blow up when those tanks got hot."

"Blown up fire fighters are not nearly as nice as whole ones." She winked at him and went out into the chaos of the yard.

He had dearly wished they were not in the middle of an inferno, he would have liked to get to know her better. He wasn't going to do that though, he never got involved with the locals. He would only be around for a few weeks, or maybe a couple of months at the most, before he got called to a new location or the fire season ended and he went back home. The way this fire continued to rage on it might just be the later, it sure didn't look like the monster would be tamed anytime soon.

The good side was that for the most part the fire had finally turned away from the few houses on the mountain, and also away from the town. It was still too unpredictable to allow the outlying residents to return until they got a nice large fire break to ensure their safety. That meant when they got to take a rest break, they could get back to the house and actually have a shower and four walls to sleep in, rather than the ground or their transport vehicle, which they had affectionately named the *Cat Box*.

He was closing in on the flare-up he'd made good time across the valley. A half hour later he shoveled dirt onto the remains of the hot area, he'd gotten the damn flare-up under control and was just finishing, so he could join his crew on the other side of the ridge.

His radio crackled. "Code 20, this is Stone. I'm hurt, feeling woozy. Got cut off from my team."

Brandon Stone, shit he's Alpha team, and one of my good buddies. They had both been rookies together and then fought on the same team for the last few summers. He knew the guy was solid, so if he was calling code 20 which stood for *Officer Assist Urgent*, he knew it was real.

He heard the superintendent radio back. "What's your 10-20 Stone?"

When Stone relayed his position co-ordinates, Trey checked the app on his phone with the map in his hand and knew he wasn't far. He heard the Alpha leader radio in his coordinates and what had separated them. Nope, he was closer and had an easier path.

He clicked his mic. "Peterson here. Super, I'm not far from him, had to double back for a flare up. I could be there in maybe fifteen to twenty minutes." He told the superintendent his coordinates.

"Affirmative. You're the closest, Peterson. Move out."

"On my way, he's just over the ridge from me. Bravo boss, you copy?"

"Roger that Trey, you're using your jaguar skills today, dude. Good luck," Bravo's crew boss, Kevin, radioed back.

Trey used his shovel as a walking stick and started hiking fast to his left. He let the radio chatter flow over him as he heard the Super find support, and keep Stone talking. He listened with half an ear, so he knew what he was going to find, but most of his concentration was on heading in as straight a line as possible to get to Brandon's location. Nothing was straight in the mountainous terrain, but he kept moving fast in the primary direction.

Fifteen minutes later he was closing in on the coordinates for where Brandon should be. Trey looked around trying to get a visual. *Fuck, where is he?* Finally, he caught sight of the yellow Nomex shirt on the ground, damn he really *was* hurt.

He ran over to him and keyed his radio. "Found him. Hey, buddy, are you okay?"

"Not really, Trey. I think I lost some blood, on my back. Branch whacked me. Didn't know it went through. Thought it was just a bump. Hurt, but was too busy trying to get back to my team."

Trey lifted him slightly to look at the damage. Blood pooled across the ground and on the shirt and pack. There was a chunk of wood sticking out of the shirt, no longer piercing the skin but still caught up in the Nomex. "Dammit, gotta get you patched up, dude. Let's get the shirt off." Trey yanked off his gloves and his pack and dropped it next to his friend. Keyed his mic again. "Super, got some blood loss. Need backup here."

"10-4 Trey. On its way, ten minutes, VLAT 1. Go with him."

"Copy."

He helped get the pack off Brandon and then the Nomex shirt and finally the t-shirt underneath, which was soaked in blood. "Yeah, man you've got some blood here. It started to clot but the t-shirt was stuck so it's back to bleeding again. I'll get that stopped."

Trey checked for any wood still in the wound and didn't find any. So, he applied pressure with one hand and yanked some salve and bandages from his first aid kit. He dressed the wound, on Brandon's shoulder just next to where the

pack strap had been. Finally, the whop-whop of the helicopter sounded in the distance, about damn time too.

The flight crew got Brandon on board, Trey grabbed up
the equipment, and climbed in too. He'd never ridden in a
Very Large Air Tanker or VLAT for short, they weren't
transport vehicles but were used to dump eleven thousand
gallons of water or fire retardant. But they would do in a
pinch, it could take an hour to get a transport helo in from
Chelan and he thought Brandon needed to be seen quicker
than that.

The medic looked Brandon over. "I think Chedwick will
do, it's closer and therefore faster, they have blood and a
good doc, no need to go into Chelan. We can go back to
dumping water quicker that way, but he'll still get good
treatment."

"Sounds good." Trey nodded and radioed the superintendent to explain the plan. The superintendent told Trey he'd
send someone down to Chedwick to pick the two of them up
in a day or two and for Trey to take some R&R while he had
the chance. Trey signed off as they landed and wondered if
he had time to have a drink with the little bombshell Mary
Ann. No, he wasn't hooking up with the locals.

They set down near the ferry landing and there was an
ambulance waiting to take them to the clinic.

CHAPTER 2

*M*ary Ann Thompson walked out of the school, it was her day to volunteer teach the kids life skills. Nearly everyone in town took one day a month to go in to teach something to the students. Some people did the older teens, and some only the grade school, and some spent the whole day instructing all the grades. She went in once a month and worked with all ages, to show them how the math they were learning in school applied to life.

Often people didn't know the purpose of certain math skills and she enjoyed showing them how to apply their math knowledge to real life. She always marveled at the fact that some grown adults never realized that they used algebra and trigonometry every day. That those x's and y's were pieces of pizza or loads of laundry or whatever. Areas and circumferences were every day measurements of rooms or pizza sizes. *Pizza again, dang, I must be hungry.* She loved to show the kids how they would really use algebra or trigonometry. Maybe not all of it, but some.

The thump-thump of a helicopter approaching drew her attention, it flew overhead toward the landing. *That's odd, why is it aiming for the dock area? Instead of the lake, to draw on water. What is it doing?* She was used to seeing them hovering over Lake Chelan to draw on water and then flying over the top of their small town of Chedwick, Washington, back and forth, between the lake and the fire to drop their load. She looked again, just to make sure. It wasn't a transport helicopter or a rescue helo, but one of the huge ones that dumped thousands of gallons of lake water. It always surprised her to see the gigantic helicopter look like a tiny gnat, next to the billows of smoke on the mountains. Sometimes you could even see the flames, and the helicopter appeared like just a speck next to them.

But she hadn't ever seen those helos land in town, she didn't even know they could set down on ground, she thought maybe they were equipped—like a seaplane—with floatation devices. Well clearly, she was wrong about that, but she couldn't imagine a reason why they would set down at the landing. *Maybe to drop someone off? But again, why would they do that?* They had vehicles up on the mountain to transport people up and down the hills. It took a while to get up there, since the road wasn't exactly smooth, but still it was only about an hour trip.

She was going in that direction anyway, so she thought maybe she could see or find out what was happening, but before she could get to the landing the helicopter took off toward the lake. She shrugged and continued on her path, past the clinic, on the way to the pizza place. The town ambulance roared down the street, slammed on the brakes and then backed into the unloading area. She skidded to a stop and watched while they hauled a hot shot out of the back on a gurney.

Her breath caught, hoping it wasn't Trey, the cute firefighter that had come to evacuate Kristen that day, a few weeks ago, when the fire was bearing down on the town.

Thank God, the winds had shifted a couple of days later and had blown the fire back in the other direction into a more remote location. Their town, and a couple of others up-lake from them, were the only settlements along this stretch of the Cascade mountains, so the fire was burning up remote wilderness, rather than homes. Trey hopped out, right after the gurney, following the medics toward the clinic, when he spotted her and dashed over.

"Hi Mary Ann, do you remember me?"

"Of course, I do, Trey. What happened?" She gestured at the ambulance.

"One of the guys got hurt when a tree gave up its fight with gravity, he'd already been cut off from his squad, due to a flare-up, and I was the closest. He lost some blood, but the medics think he'll be fine."

"That's good, I'm glad it's not you." Glory be, the man looked fine even all dirty and hairy. She'd never thought about the fact they wouldn't have running water to shave and shower while they were out in the field. He smelled like smoke and carried a ton of gear, probably for him and his hurt teammate.

"Yeah, me too. Say, I'll probably be here in town tonight and maybe tomorrow. Want to meet up at the bar later for a drink? I promised you one, as I recall."

She blushed, remembering their first meet when she'd been so flirty in the midst of a crisis. "That would be great. I can meet you at Greg's bar. I'm going to the pizza place, Antonio's, want me to save you a slice?"

"Sure, I'll probably stick here for an hour, to make sure my buddy is okay." He rubbed at his beard. "Then I'll go by the fire station where I can get cleaned up, we left some clothes there. So maybe an hour and a half, or two?"

She beamed at him. "Sounds good. I'll see you in a while."

Mary Ann decided to go home so she could shower and

change, then she wouldn't feel hot and tired from teaching kids all day. Afterward she could pick up the pizza, so it would be hot for her to share with Trey. She frowned. Greg wouldn't mind them bringing in outside food. He didn't make his money off the fried foods he offered, it was simply a way to keep people from getting too drunk on empty stomachs. She had dated Greg in high school and knew he was low-key about things like that.

She waved to a neighbor as she turned onto her street. She'd even waitressed for a while at Greg's before she started working with Kristen on the jewelry. She hadn't minded the job, it paid the bills, and she enjoyed people, for the most part, as long as they didn't get too drunk and handsy. Greg ran a tight ship, and he was a big guy with an intensity that people just didn't want to tangle with, so it was a calm place for a bar.

She was happy not to be working there anymore though, the jewelry work was a way better job, and it was so fulfilling to create things from metal. Even when all she was doing was the cleanup work on the charms for the *Adventures with Tsilly* game, it had been a fun job. Now that Kristen was teaching her how to do more, it was darn near a miracle position. She had some ideas for items she'd like to make, but she wasn't going to mention those until Kristen was done showing her everything else. Someday she might like to try out her ideas, but thinking about working on her own gave her chills, she didn't know enough yet.

When that jewelry designer had rambled into town one day a dozen years ago, and had stuck around long enough to teach some classes, Mary Ann had taken them as had Kristen. But Kristen was a few years older and had been in high school, so he might have taught the older kids more than he did middle school students. Mary Ann hadn't kept up with it like Kristen had, and she didn't feel like she had the same

SHIRLEY PENICK

talent that Kristen did, but she was learning and practicing and having a wonderful time doing so.

She got home and went straight for the shower peeling off her jeans and top as she went. Thinking the whole way about what she wanted to wear to meet with Trey. He had such beautiful eyes, a dark chocolate brown. Great eyebrows framed his eyes and drew a woman into their depths. He had a nice face too, and a warm smile, so far, she'd only seen him with a scruffy beard and his firefighter clothes on, which were bulky. She didn't know much else, his hair color was brown, but she didn't know if it was light or dark. It was a mystery since it had always been in a helmet with just a little showing.

She dried off and flipped through her sundresses trying to find just the right one. It was still warm in the evening, so a sundress would be pretty and cool. Hmm, the blue one with the lace, or the pink one with the flower embroidery, or there was the white eyelet, or her go-to black flowered one? *Okay starting to make myself crazy, I need to just pick a flippin' dress, the man's only seen me in dirty pants and t-shirts, anything will be better than that.* Deciding on the blue one, she put it on with some strappy sandals, and spritzed on some perfume. She curled her hair and fluffed it to look carefree, then put on makeup to make her eyes bigger and her mouth hot. He'd only seen her all dirty and disheveled, so she wanted to wow him.

The pizza was ready for her, all boxed up and hot. She'd decided on a meat-lovers since most men were basically carnivores, and to appease her guilty conscience there were mushrooms and olives to give a nod to vegetables. After ordering it she'd given Greg a call just to give him a heads-up that she was about to carry in pizza to share with Trey. Greg had been glad to hear one of the hotshots was in town and would be in his place. He really did want to give them all a beer on the house, for taking care of Kristen the day of the evacuation.

She breezed into the bar with her pizza and glanced around, she didn't see Trey anywhere. Finding a table near the door she put the box down. The waitress cruised up with plates, napkins and silverware, so apparently, Greg had spread the word.

"What can I get you to drink, hon?"

"I think a Long Island Iced Tea would be nice. I can pretend I'm behaving and not drinking a boatload of alcohol."

Her friend laughed. "Providing you don't have too many of them, girl."

TREY WAS CHILLIN' in the waiting room, when the doc came out. Trey clicked off his phone, stood up and started toward the man, who waved him back to his seat and came over to sit next to him.

"I'm Doctor Sorenson, you will be happy to hear that Brandon is going to be fine. We had to put a couple dozen stitches into him and give him some blood, but I don't foresee any problems. We'll keep him here overnight for observation, and I'd like to see him in a day or two just to check. Afterwards he can go on back up the mountain on light duty."

Trey frowned. "That shouldn't be a problem, someone needs to man the radio and coordinate teams, might as well be Brandon, he's been on the job long enough to handle it. It might tick him off to be benched, but too bad."

"Excellent, you can go in and see him for a minute if you want, but he's groggy and needs to sleep. He did lose a fair amount of blood, and rest is the best medicine at this point. You got him in here in good time, so I think he will be fine."

"I'll just stick my head in, so he knows I checked on him and head out. I'm going to go have a beer at Greg's place."

The doctor nodded. "I saw you talking to Mary Ann when the paramedics brought Brandon in."

"Um, yeah, she's going to save me a slice of pizza." He rubbed a hand over his neck slightly embarrassed to be caught chatting up a local.

"She's a good girl. I'll see you tomorrow." Then the man was gone leaving Trey to stare after him.

Trey went down the hall toward where the doctor had directed him and stuck his head in the door. Brandon was hooked up to machines and had his eyes shut. It freaked him out a little to see his friend down. Trey didn't want to wake him if he was asleep, so he went in quietly, over to the bed and whispered. "You awake, buddy?"

Brandon opened his eyes slowly with what looked like great effort. "Kinda."

"Yeah, the doc said you would be out of it, so I'm going to let you sleep, he only wants to keep you overnight. Said you could go back up the mountain on light duty in a day or two."

"Shit, baby-sitting the radio and sticking pins in a map. Not what I signed on for."

"Better than being sent home... or worse," Trey reminded his friend. And he was damn glad he had the chance to remind him, he'd had more than enough time to worry about his friend in the twenty minutes it had taken him to get to Brandon. And then finding him on the ground and bleeding had not helped his peace of mind.

"True. Thanks for saving my ass, man."

Trey shrugged. "You'd have done the same."

"Of course, but I still appreciate it."

Not wanting to get maudlin he changed the subject. "I'll

be back in the morning Brandon, get some rest. I think I'll head over to the local watering hole for a beer."

Brandon sighed. "Aw man, I wish I could join you, I could use a cold one."

"Yeah, not tonight buddy, you need to let those antibiotics kick in and kill any infection that tree tried to give you."

"True, and I am kinda tired." His eyes started drooping and Trey knew his friend was not going to stay awake much longer.

"Later dude." Trey fist bumped Brandon.

Brandon slurred, "Later," and his eyes closed.

Trey knew his teammate was good for the night, so he walked down the hall and out into the summer evening. He wanted to find the fire department to shower and change. Then he would feel up to meeting with Mary Ann. Hot woman, pizza and a beer, what more could a man ask for? Having a home base in town was helpful too, the local fire department was all volunteer, so it's not like they had a dormitory to sleep in, but it had a small area for them to crash, a shower and kitchen, so he could stay a day or two, until the superintendent sent someone down to get him. He headed toward the cop shop, the dispatcher was supposed to have a spare key he could use to get in.

He walked into the police department and nearly ran into the officer he'd met during the evacuation. "Hey Nolan, howzit?"

Nolan looked up and grinned. "Good, Trey, what brings you to town?"

"Oh, one of the guys got hurt, and we had to bring him in for some stitches. They're keeping him overnight, just to be on the safe side."

"Glad to hear he'll be okay." Nolan asked, "Are you going to crash at the firehouse?"

Trey shrugged. "Yeah, they said the dispatcher has a spare key I can use."

"That she does. Go over there to the left, she's behind the glass, let her know what you're after and she'll check you one out."

"Thanks, see you around."

Trey walked over to where Nolan had indicated and looked through what was clearly bullet-proof glass. He thought that might be a bit of overkill for this tiny town, but nobody asked him. He waved at the dispatcher, he was surprised to see it was a woman about his age, for some reason he always thought of dispatchers as being cranky old women. This one was quite pretty.

"Hello, what can I help you with?" the dispatcher asked.

"I'm Trey Peterson, one of the forest fire fighters."

"Oh, you're one of the ones that got Kristen evacuated aren't you. I heard all about it. Thanks for saving our Kristen, she makes all my jewelry, and I would be devastated if she was hurt or blown up." She waved her hand toward a very pretty necklace which was a black rectangular stone with stripes of white through it, set in a silver frame with a large pearl dangling from the bottom.

"Yeah, blown up residents is not our favorite scenario."

"So, do you want a key to the firehouse, so you can get cleaned up before you meet Mary Ann for pizza at Greg's?"

Trey felt himself start. *How in the hell does she know, it has barely been an hour since I talked to Mary Ann.*

The dispatcher laughed at his expression and shrugged. "Small towns, you'll get used to it, if you stick around a while."

He wasn't sure he would ever get used to that, but he didn't argue.

She pushed a clipboard under the window. "Just sign your

name below and your unit number. And I'll need a quick copy of your driver's license just for protocol."

He marveled that she would want proof of ID when she knew where and what and with whom he was having dinner. He signed his name and passed his license under the glass. She gave him a key and a small map of the town, there was a big X on the fire department and she had circled Greg's bar and there was a little star on the police department. No way was he getting lost.

He tried to wipe the grin off his face as he looked back at the dispatcher. "Thanks."

She smiled. "Have fun with Mary Ann tonight."

CHAPTER 3

Mary Ann took a sip of her Long Island Iced Tea and almost choked on it. Trey had just ambled in the door, and man did that boy clean up well. He had dark brown hair that was still damp from his shower. He was clean shaven for the first time and had on jeans and a black t-shirt that fit him like skin. And glory-be, did he have a nice build. She was nearly salivating watching him scan the bar, a couple of people pointed towards her and that embarrassed the crap out of her. What was he going to think about that?

But then his gaze locked on her, and a smile spread across his face which made his eyes twinkle, and she didn't care what he thought about her nosey neighbors anymore, because she couldn't think at all. He sauntered over to her as her mouth dried up, dear God he was sex on a stick. But she managed to smile at him, she couldn't stand or move yet, but she did manage a smile.

He slid into the chair next to hers at the table and took her hand. "You sure do look pretty tonight."

"Thanks, you look pretty good yourself." Good grief, did

she just say that to him? She was glad the bar had dim lighting, so maybe he wouldn't see her face flame with heat.

He laughed. "I guess we've mostly seen each other at our worst. You've got beautiful hair."

"I've never seen yours at all, it's always been in a helmet." That was a stupid thing to say so she fumbled with the pizza box. "Here have some pizza, it's still hot, I only got it a few minutes ago."

"It smells delicious, thanks."

Greg walked up and slapped him on the shoulder. "You managed to make it in, can I get you a beer or something to drink. First one's on the house for saving Kristen and Mary Ann, here."

"Sure, do you have any Guinness?"

"Certainly. No self-respecting bar would be without it. I'll be right back."

Greg strode away, and Trey took a slice of pizza, put it on his plate and then slid one over onto her plate, also. "Meat lovers, huh? What if I was a vegetarian?"

"You're a forest fire fighter, I doubt you have the luxury to be a vegetarian, I imagine you eat whatever is handy including MREs, those supposed Meals Ready to Eat, and jerky."

He laughed, and she thought it was a wonderful sound. Deep and throaty. Yumm. "You're right of course, and I never met a piece of meat I wasn't happy to devour. MREs aren't bad the first day or two, but after that they get old pretty quick. So, good call on both the pizza and the meat lovers." He took a big bite and hummed in appreciation and Mary Ann's stomach muscles tightened at the sound. She needed to get a grip, he was just eating for goodness sake.

Greg came back and set the beer down on the table, all dark and frosty in the glass. "Enjoy your meal and let one of the girls know when you need a refill."

Trey nodded, since his mouth was full of pizza, and Greg went back behind the bar.

Trey took a swallow of his beer and Mary Ann just watched in thrall as his throat worked. She had to get hold of herself, it was like she had never seen a man before. This was becoming ridiculous.

Oh, for goodness sake, knock it off already and stop drooling, you're making an ass out of yourself. "So, what do you do in the off season?"

"I'm a web designer, I work for myself and do freelance for other people."

That did it. "Really? We need a web designer; the whole town has been talking about updating our web presence to bring in more tourists. So few people even know we exist, let alone all the things our town has to offer. We had a big meeting in January to try to figure out how to build tourism and one of the key issues was a better web focus. Chris got the amusement park up and we've been so busy keeping up with that, the web pages fell by the wayside. But we still need it, if you get a chance while you're in town you might talk to some people to see if they can get on your list..."

TREY JUST SAT THERE STARING at her as she went on and on about web pages, he wasn't sure he heard much of what she was saying. She was so animated about it, her green eyes were sparkling, and she had taken his hand in her soft warm ones, he couldn't think or move, let alone pay attention. The woman was tying him in knots, and she had no idea. He as a rule didn't get involved with locals, he was only going to be here a couple of months, and even that was mostly spent up on the mountain fighting fires. So, no he couldn't get involved with her no matter how much he wanted to. Not a good idea.

He cleared his throat and removed his hand from hers, in an effort to get himself under control. A long drink of beer might help him to cool down, he grabbed it like a lifeline and drank deep. There had to be something else to focus on, he glanced around frantically to see if there was something they could do, maybe with other people. He hadn't really looked at the local watering hole when he'd come in, he'd had one thing on his mind and that was the woman he was currently trying to distance himself from.

It was a typical place with a mirror behind the bar displaying several rows of hard liquor. There was lots of wood molding around the mirror, that you didn't see much of these days. In front of the bar were a dozen stools made of curved wood with tan seats, they looked older but in good condition. One wall was old bricks in what looked like archways, he wondered if they were real archways that had been bricked in, or just designed to look like that. The back room was very different, and he wondered if it was added on at a later time, or if two different spaces had been merged. The room where the pool tables were had big windows that looked out into a green space. Lots of trees could be seen through the wall of windows and he wondered if the glass was tinted from the outside to make it hard to see in.

Was there something they could do to keep his mind off of her? Two pool tables were going strong, but they were both in the middle of a game with quarters stacked up for more rounds. There seemed to be a rowdy group of people playing darts, but it looked like a competition. There were a few people dancing on the tiny dance floor to a rowdy country song. That would work.

"Would you like to dance?"

She blinked and looked at the people on the floor flailing about. "Um sure, I guess. I'm not a great dancer."

"Perfect, neither am I." He smiled and stood. She followed him, and he started flailing about too, which made her laugh. That lightened the mood, and he began to get his equilibrium back. Just as the song switched. To a slow ballad. Dammit.

She smiled a shy smile and moved toward him, he could do nothing, but open his arms. She moved in close, and they shuffled. She smelled like heaven, and her body fit his like they were made for each other. Her head fit right under his chin, and her soft curves just about did him in. Desire pounded through him and all he could think about was taking a taste of her soft lips. He had to do something and kissing her was not the right thing to do, even if that's all he could think about.

She sighed, and he was lost, adrift in the sensuality of the moment. He let himself hold her close for just the length of the song, then he would do something to get them back on the right track. What he would do, he had no idea, but something. Anything. The song finally ended, and he stepped back as another slow ballad came on. Dear God, were they trying to kill him? He looked down at her and wanted to put his mouth on hers, so bad he could almost taste her already. And she was staring at his mouth like he was a nice tasty snack.

His brain scrambled for a distraction, he had to get away, out of the danger zone. Bathroom, yeah that would work. "Want to order us a refill? I'll be right back." He left her to find her own way back to the table, he couldn't be his normal gentlemanly self, he had to separate from her before he fell into her warmth.

When he got to the bathroom, his mind whirled with what to do. If he stayed with her any longer he would end up doing something stupid. But what excuse could he use? He'd been up on the mountain so long his social skills were sorely lacking. *Aha, fatigue, that will work.* He could claim he was exhausted and needed sleep. She would feel sorry for him and let him escape. He couldn't be too obvious though, maybe eat another slice of pizza and yawn, yeah that would work. He straightened his shoulders and went out to implement his plan.

CHAPTER 4

rey woke suddenly when he heard a sharp tone coming from his right. He reared up and looked around blearily. What in the hell was that noise? Where in the hell was he? Then he heard the dispatcher calmly speak, calling out a kitchen fire and the address. He remembered he was at the fire station in the small town of Chedwick Washington. They only had a volunteer fire fighting crew, so the shrill tone had been the wake-up call for the citizens that were part of the force.

He scrubbed a hand over his face and decided to slide his jeans back on, since he had no idea what the protocol was and how many guys would show up. He looked at his phone and saw it was four in the morning and he wondered who would be up in the kitchen at that time.

He hadn't been asleep very long, since he'd had to spend hours trying to get his body to calm down after spending the evening with Mary Ann. And he had berated himself for running out on her, like a damn chickenshit. He had spent most of the night alternating between thinking it was a smart move on his part to get away from her, and wishing he'd hung on close and taken a taste of her sweet lips. She'd looked so disappointed when he'd feigned exhaustion and fled the scene. Now he really was exhausted from his dithering all night and yes, he was aware that was an old grandma word, but the fact of the matter is that he had been dithering. And he couldn't deny it or put a better label on it.

He heard cars pull into the parking lot and the guys go into the equipment bays underneath him and take out the trucks. Two engines rumbled to life and they pulled out of the building, but they didn't turn on their sirens. He could see the lights flash through the windows, but it was a quiet exit. He listened to the radio as a couple other cars pulled into the parking lot and he heard feet on the stairs leading up to him. The chatter on the radio sounded like this kitchen fire was not too threatening and they radioed that they would not need any other assistance.

Two guys came into the room and didn't look at all surprised to see him. One of them he had met the day of the evacuation, but he didn't remember his name.

The guy smiled at him and walked over with his hand out to shake his. "Trey, isn't it? We met a couple of weeks ago when you helped Kristen with the tanks. I'm Chris, Kristen's brother-in-law. And this here is Scott Davidson, the pastor in town."

"Nice to meet you Scott," Trey said as he shook hands with both men.

Scott smiled. "Nice to meet you too, Trey. Didn't I see you at Greg's place tonight or rather last night with Mary Ann?"

Damn this is such a small town. "Yes, I did have some pizza and beer with the lady. I can't say that I noticed you there."

"I was playing darts with the local enthusiasts. We have a tournament every couple of weeks."

Chris laughed. "Yeah if that's what you want to call it. I

think it's just an excuse to drink beer and throw pointy objects."

"Same, same," Scott said with a shrug. "We better get the coffee on before the rest of the guys get here, you know they'll be bringing day-old pastries with them from Samantha's place."

Trey followed the guys into the kitchen area and leaned against the counter as he watched the two men work together, with an efficiency born of a longtime friendship.

"My bet's on burned butter and her *helper* panicking, what's yours?" Chris asked as he turned the oven on to preheat.

"Could be, and he most likely made matters worse by throwing sugar on the hot stuff instead of flour or putting the lid on the pan and turning off the heat. But my money's on the donut fryer and him pulling the fire alarm rather than using the *new-fangled* suppression system. Why Samantha lets him stay is beyond me." Scott took the coffee off the shelves and measured it into the large coffee maker's basket.

Chris grinned as he filled the pot with water. "You're right, it is about donut finishing time, isn't it? She just has a soft heart and can't bring herself to give him the heave ho. It's been six weeks since we've been called to her place at four in the morning."

"Yeah that's because she's been getting in before he gets there. Last night she was at Greg's. She and Kyle were burning up the dance floor. She probably didn't make it in as quick as she normally does, and he started without her."

"That makes sense, she hasn't been out on the town in weeks." Chris nodded.

Scott plugged in the coffee pot. "No, she hasn't. I don't think she's taking any classes this summer, so she probably decided to have a little fun."

"Right. Having no classes is like being let out of jail, I'm so glad I finally graduated. But now Samantha will pull back again...."

They both stopped speaking when the radio crackled to life, the trucks were signing in to indicate they were on their way back. Chris and Scott hustled around the kitchen getting out large baking sheets, cups and plates, sugar and cream for coffee and butter, lots of butter.

Trey heard the trucks pull back into the station, followed by feet on the stairs. The first guy in the door he didn't recognize, but the two giant bakery boxes he carried made Trey's mouth water. Some other guys streamed in, one of which was also carrying two large bakery boxes. *Feast time!*

The baking trays were loaded with all kinds of delicious-looking pastries from the first two boxes and put into the oven. The second two boxes held still-warm donuts. Fire-fighters, both men and women continued to stream in the door. While the pastries heated, they all made themselves coffee and chowed down on the donuts.

Chris asked, "Donut fryer or butter?"

"Donut fryer," they all answered in unison.

Scott laughed. "I win."

Greg came in last and slapped Trey on the shoulder. "Hey Trey, good to see you. Kind of surprised you're here, not that Mary Ann is easy, but she seemed to be really interested, last night."

"Oh, well, I don't hook up with local girls when I'm out on a hotshot location."

Greg guffawed, "Seriously? Why the hell not?"

The room had turned deadly quiet and all eyes were on him. "Well I just don't want to get involved, knowing I'm only in town for a few weeks. I don't normally even go out for a beer like I did with Mary Ann. I just keep to myself, I don't want anyone getting hurt by my leaving."

One of the women snorted. "Well you're a cutie, but

you're not all that. I'm sure we delicate little females could manage to live, even after you left."

Everyone laughed at that and then turned back to their breakfast extravaganza, leaving Trey to wonder if maybe he was being a bit on the conceited side. He and Mary Ann had exchanged phone numbers before parting ways, he wondered if he should call her. He'd have to wait and see how his day went.

CHAPTER 5

*M*ary Ann frowned as she thought about her evening with Trey last night. He'd gotten distant after their dance, she wondered what had happened. She'd been having a great time, and he seemed to be into her, too. For a moment on the dance floor she was sure he was going to kiss her, but that was when he pulled back. *Why do men have to be so weird? I just don't understand them. It's not like I'm married... Oh, I wonder if he's married?* He didn't act like it, but some men didn't ever give off the married vibe.

Well she wasn't going to worry about it, Kristen wanted to teach her some new techniques today and that was exciting. She loved learning new things. One day she would be good enough to create her own ideas.

A few hours later, Mary Ann was practicing soldering. Kristen had shown her how to do it and then given her several challenges to try. It was fun. Although, she'd totally destroyed one of them, when she had held the flame on a little too long. It was now a glob of metal. Kristen had laughed and told her it was all part of the learning process. That some work needed a very light touch of the torch and some needed much more heat. She was concentrating on a second try at the one she'd melted beyond recognition when someone knocked on the door. She started and ruined the second one. Drat.

She clicked off the torch and turned to see Kristen let Gus Ferguson into the studio. It had only recently come out that Gus was loaded, he had helped some people out from time to time on the down low. But when he had financed the amusement park, it had been revealed that he had millions. Not that Gus handed it out willy-nilly. He carefully selected people who needed help with their businesses and put his money where his mouth was. Although he could be pushy when he got his mind on something.

Gus nodded and walked in. "Kristen, how ya doing? So, I've been hearing about your new studio, looks mighty nice."

"Um thanks, Gus. I like it," Kristen said looking nervous.

Gus nodded in Mary Ann's direction and she smiled back at him. Turning back to Kristen he said, "So I hear there's a nice gallery space on the first floor of the house, too."

Now Kristen looked really panicked. "Um, yes, there is a nice area, but…"

"So, are ya going to be helping the town by opening a gallery to show off all the goods we make here?" Gus asked her in his way, firm but laid back.

"Um, I don't really have the personality to run a gallery. I need a whole lot more solitude than that and I plan to head back up the mountain as soon as it's safe."

"But ya could open it and let someone else run it. You've got the space and a good amount of your own things to put in. Seems to me Mary Ann here could work on charms and the like, while she manned the gallery and waited for folks to show up." Looking at Mary Ann he asked, "Would ya like that?"

Oh, no. She was not getting in the middle of this. "Yes, I

would, but it's Kristen's house and she still needs to be happy and comfortable with the idea. And not feel railroaded into it, Gus." She put her hands on her hips and felt like shaking her finger at him.

"Oh, not railroading, just asking some questions and maybe hinting a little bit."

Kristen said tightly, "I'll give it some serious consideration."

"Good enough, I'm going to mosey along. Good day to ya ladies."

Kristen didn't say anything, she just stood there stiff as a board. When he was out of earshot she exploded. "Damn it. I don't want a gallery. But every person I've talked to thinks it would be awesome. Fine, you, Mary Ann, can open the gallery. I don't want to have anything, at all, to do with it, besides stocking it with my work. You set it up. You figure it out. You deal with it, start to finish. I provide the space and my work."

Shocked at Kristen's attitude, she felt a grin slide over her features. Mary Ann tried not to let it show, but that was no use, she was thrilled with the idea. "Yay! You won't regret it. I promise."

"No, I'm sure I will regret it, but I don't want someone coming by my studio every day asking about a gallery. So just do it."

"Okay," she said and then started thinking about all the things she didn't know about running a gallery and felt panic slide into her.

Kristen folded her arms across her chest and narrowed her eyes. "Spill it."

"I do have a few questions about it. For instance, is there some kind of contract for taking things on consignment? Do we make the sale and pay all the taxes and then pay the artists? Or do they pay the taxes and we are just the medium for the sale? Questions like that."

"Oh, you don't need to be worried about that, I have my jewelry in other galleries, so I already have a contract we can use. Some of the more abstract stuff is what I worry about. Like do we need to advertise? Do we have to have a web presence? Can we just let the town put us in the brochure and website they are creating, or will we have to take the time to figure all that out? What should we name it? Will we need to hire more people or just open it a few hours each day? What if you get sick?"

Wow, Kristen had even more questions than she did, she laughed nervously. "Okay, so it's not quite as simple as gathering a few items and unlocking the door, but it can't be too hard. Are any of the galleries you work with on friendly enough terms to ask?"

Kristen shook her head and then stopped and frowned. "You know, Nolan Thompson's mother has a gallery for her art, so he might have some ideas or knowledge."

"Really? What kind of art?"

"Glass, Lucille Thompson."

Mary Ann's mouth dropped open in shock and her breath caught. "Are you kidding? Lucille Thompson is Nolan's mother? I love her stuff. She has to be my favorite, since we have the same last name."

"Not kidding, and he even has his own glass sculpting equipment in storage. He says he knows the mechanics but isn't creative, I'm not sure I believe him"

"Wow, that's amazing." Mary Ann felt tingles run over her. "Maybe we could get a few of her pieces too, wouldn't that be awesome?"

"I'll get in touch with him and see what he has to say."

"That would be so cool." She looked back at her soldering practice and thought about all her ideas and questions. "I'm wondering if I should keep practicing what you taught me this morning or sit down and make some lists and plans. It will be an eclectic assortment of artists and art."

"True, not your normal gallery for certain."

"Normal is overrated and usually just a bunch of lies anyway. I think it will be fun." She slid her gaze over to Kristen. "So, you're getting pretty chummy with the new police officer."

She saw a slight flush on Kristen's face as she waved her hand in dismissal. "Just friends. Any word from the hotshots on the fire?"

Now it was Mary Ann's turn to be put on the spot. "Not much, Trey came into town yesterday. One of the guys had gotten hurt and needed to be seen by the doctor. He'd lost some blood, and I hear he was kind of pale by the time they got him here. But the doc fixed him up and he'll be going back on the line in a few days."

"Trey, huh, are you getting chummy with Trey?"

She shook her head sadly. "Boy, I'd love that, he is a hunk. We had some laughs at Greg's bar, but then he said he needed to go and I didn't even get a kiss. What's wrong with these guys, they can't even spare a little lip-lock."

"Um, I have no idea," Kristen said, but she was looking around guiltily.

Mary Ann was no fool, she put her hands on her hips. "Kristen, have you been making out with the new cop in town?"

"I have nothing to say." She crossed her arms over her chest.

Mary Ann laughed. "You have! And you've been holding out. Let's hear the deets."

This time when Kristen blushed her whole face turned bright red. "Just a kiss or two, no big deal really."

Mary Ann lifted an eyebrow. "Then why are you seven shades of red?"

"I repeat, I have nothing to tell."

"Well, let me just say. You go girl!"

"Mary Ann, you are incorrigible." Kristen folded her arms and shook her head.

No, just jealous as hell. "And not nearly as lucky as you, so I'll just have to live vicariously."

"Or grab Trey the next time he's in town and lay a big fat one on him."

She shook her head. "Oh, I couldn't do that."

"Why not? It works like a charm."

She started at that. "What? Are you telling me you grabbed Officer Thompson and kissed him?"

"Maybe."

"Whoo hoo, you are totally my hero!" She clapped her hands and then put them on her hips. "And here you are pretending to be this shy little recluse."

Kristen shook her head. "Not shy; just not a *bunch of people at the same time* person, and I have to work alone to get the creative juices flowing."

Mary Ann grinned at her. "I think I need to tap into your mysterious charisma and encourage the hottie firefighter to give me a little smooch."

"You go right ahead." Kristen shrugged. "But it's really just grabbing him and kissing him. Most men don't need too much encouragement. Just a nice solid hint, or in this case, a kiss."

"I bow to your expertise and wisdom."

"Okay, play time is over, back to work."

"Yes, ma'am." Mary Ann was going to work, but she was also going to think about grabbing Trey and laying a big fat one on him, next time she saw him.

CHAPTER 6

*T*rey didn't get a chance to call Mary Ann back, his superintendent called him at eight in the morning. After all the guys had left the station, he'd drifted off to sleep with his belly full of pastries, so the call woke him. After that he had to get moving. They needed him back on the line immediately and one of the cops in town had volunteered to take him back up the mountain. He showered, dressed, grabbed a last cup of cold coffee and hustled over to check on Brandon.

Trey walked into the room Brandon was in and set his gear down by the door. "How are you feeling?"

"Like I got run over by a truck. No, really, not bad, shoulder hurts like a mother, but that's to be expected. No word on when I'm getting out. You've got your gear with you, are you heading out?"

Trey nodded. "Yeah, the super called a little while ago, the damn wind changed again, and the monster is turning back toward the town, through that valley it missed the first time. So, we're all headed to that."

"Fuck, and here I am laid up."

"Can't do anything about that, shit happens. You just work on getting better, do what the doc says, and you'll be back soon."

Brandon frowned. "Yeah to man the radios."

"Somebody's gotta. It won't be for long. I left your gear in a locker at the fire department, number forty-five. Gotta get moving, see you soon."

"Later."

Trey grabbed up his gear and was on his way to the police station to turn in the key and catch a ride back up the mountain. He decided to text Mary Ann to tell her he was going back up to the fire and that he'd see her again.

MARY ANN SMILED as she thought about the text Trey had sent her yesterday, he'd said he was sorry he'd cut their evening short and hoped to see her next time he was in town. He'd said he had to go back on the line immediately since the wind had shifted again. He'd sent her a tiny picture of wind blowing a cloud. She'd texted him back "stay safe" with a tiny flame and a picture of a volcano because she thought it had looked like fire on the mountain. He'd texted her back a thumbs-up and a fire truck. It was silly, but fun, too.

She breezed into Samantha's bakery, she wanted some pastries to take with her to Kristen's, she hadn't gotten to eat breakfast because she'd been too busy answering her phone, clearly the word had gotten out about the gallery.

Samantha was behind the counter since most of the baking was done for the day. Mary Ann was glad she wasn't a baker because getting up hours before the sun rose in order to have breakfast foods and bread ready for an early morning crowd, would kill her. She was not a morning person. Fortunately, Samantha was.

Samantha smiled. "Well hello Miss Gallery Curator, what brings you to my humble store this morning."

"Breakfast, my phone has not stopped ringing. Did Gus put an announcement in the newspaper or tone it out over the fire radio? Just how does everyone already know about the gallery opening?"

"You've lived here all your life, you know how fast the grapevine works."

"Well yeah, but it hasn't even been twenty-four hours."

Samantha laughed. "All it takes is one meal, and wasn't Gus there in the morning yesterday? That's a good three meals in my book, plenty of time for the word to get out."

Mary Ann shook her head. "But Kristen didn't even agree to it while Gus was still there. Did he bug the studio? Have spies? Hang around and eavesdrop? How did he know?"

"Don't you worry your pretty little head about it, it's not important in the grand scheme of things. What can I box up for you?"

By the time she was done the box was brimming with sugary goodness, she'd gone a little crazy, maybe she could share with Barbara and the ladies at the shop next door. While Samantha was taping the box shut, so Mary Ann could get it out the door without it exploding, Theresa flounced in the bakery.

"Oh, Mary Ann, there you are, poor thing, consoling yourself with donuts I see. Bless your heart, don't take it personally, I'm sure he meant all women, not just you."

"What are you talking about, Theresa?"

Theresa put her hand on her ample bosom that was about to explode right out of her sundress. "Oh, you haven't heard, I just assumed with you buying out half the store that you were depression eating. After all, if Trey is dead set against hooking up with the locals, I just assumed..."

Samantha set a to-go coffee cup on the counter. "Here's your coffee Theresa, I'm sure you're in a rush like usual."

"Oh yes of course, I do have to get to work. Bye, ladies." She smirked at Mary Ann as she turned toward the exit.

Once the door was shut Samantha said, "What a bitch."

"What in the hell was she talking about?"

"Oh, just fire department chatter. I heard the guys were giving Trey a hard time about bailing on you the other night. He said something about not hooking up with locals because he was only in town a short time and didn't want any hard feelings when he left. He told them it was very unusual for him to even go out for a beer."

Ah, so that's why he'd backpedaled after looking like he wanted to kiss her. "That's kind of a douche-y thing to say."

"Yeah one of the female firefighters basically told him that. I didn't hear who said it, just that everyone thought it was hilarious."

Mary Ann's phone buzzed with an incoming text, she looked at it. "Hmm speak of the devil, he just sent me a picture of the fire. Why is he texting me if he doesn't "get involved" with locals? Well I'm not going to answer him, let him stew in his "don't hook up with locals" juices."

"Good for you."

Mary Ann shut the text app and saw she had three missed calls. She'd turned her ringer off in the bakery, she grimaced at the display and decided she didn't have time to think about Trey and his hoity-toity attitude, she had work to do. "Well duty calls, and calls, and calls, guess I better go answer it. See ya." She slid the bakery box into the front seat of her Chevy Aveo and hopped in to drive to Kristen's.

CHAPTER 7

*M*ary Ann was shocked at the number of calls she was receiving about the gallery opening. Her phone had never had that many calls. It rang again, and she felt like throwing it out the car window. But it was Kristen's face on the display, so she answered it.

"Mary Ann, we have to do something, my damn phone won't stop ringing. Everyone and their mother, brother, aunt and uncle are calling me to find out about the gallery. We have got to get a gallery phone like yesterday."

"Well hello to you too Kristen, and yes I know, mine is going wild too. I'll call the phone company."

"Good and can you just plan to sort of be here all the time for a week or two? You can answer both my phone and yours. It's making me crazy and for the most part all I'm doing is telling them to contact my lawyer to fill out the paperwork and bring in some samples. Since you'll be doing most of the vetting and gallery setup, I want them to co-ordinate with your schedule."

So that's why her phone was ringing off the hook. Kristen was pushing all the calls and all the responsibility toward her. She supposed that's what she'd signed up to do. "I gathered that since many of the people calling me are asking about my schedule."

"Oh, I guess I did tell some of them they would have to talk to you. Sorry. Well not really, since that got them off my phone, but…"

Mary Ann laughed. "At least you're honest. Yes, I will plan to hang around as much as possible, in fact I just picked us up some pastries from Samantha's."

"Thank God. I still have a bunch of commission pieces I need to finish, and I don't like dealing with all these people. That's your job."

Mary Ann called the phone company as soon as she hung up from talking to Kristen and the man on the phone said he would have someone come out on the ferry the next day to do the installation.

When she got to the studio she saw Kristen had put her phone outside the studio door, on a stool, she picked it up and saw a half dozen missed calls all with messages. She shook her head and went in.

Kristen turned to her and saw the phone in her hand. "Oh, no you don't. You just keep that evil torture device from hell away from me."

Mary Ann laughed. "Don't worry. I'll take care of it, but you have to give me your screen unlock code and voicemail password." She took the bakery box over and opened it. "The phone company will be here tomorrow, but we need a name for the gallery. I just pretended I was you, to order the service."

"I don't give a damn what we call it, how about *Pain in My Ass Gallery*?" Kristen took a huge bite of the chocolate donut she had snagged.

"Catchy, but not quite the impression we want the world to see. I've got some ideas. How about Artisan's Paradise, or

Serendipity, or Esoterica, or Treasures? Or what about Need it - Want it - Desire it, or Explorers, or Art on the Town, or Creative Experience? Maybe the This and That Gallery, or Eclectic Collection, or Extravaganza, or Inspirations, or Abstract Expressions?"

Kristen laughed and held up her hands. "Stop that's too many choices and a lot of good ones. You've been thinking about this. Maybe we should pick something that would go with Barbara's Adventures. Since we're the only two Victorian houses with shops in them on the street, it would be cute to match the signs and have complimentary names. Um, I think I like Explorers or Treasures the best. Terry could make us a sign that's similar to Barbara's. For Treasures, it would be a treasure chest in the bottom corner and a line of paint swirling around like her thread does, leading up to a paint brush in the top corner."

Mary Ann nodded. "For Explorers, it could still have a treasure chest but with little foot-prints leading to a magnifying glass in the top corner."

"Oh, I like them both, you decide and surprise me."

"You got it." Kristen's phone rang, and Mary Ann looked at the display. "Well speak of the devil." She answered the phone. "Hi, Terry. This is Mary Ann, Kristen threw her phone in the yard because so many people were calling. Were your ears burning, we were just talking about you?"

Kristen handed her a piece of paper with the phone passwords on it and the bakery box and made a get out of here gesture, so Mary Ann took both phones with her and went toward the gallery space, while she explained to Terry what they wanted for their sign.

Mary Ann spent the rest of the day answering phone calls, returning messages and setting up times for the artisans to bring in their items. She needed to look them over to see if they were up to the standards for the gallery.

People started coming in that very afternoon. So far everything she'd seen was excellent and she started making a sketch as to where she planned to put it all. She was having so much fun, but it was getting a little overwhelming, with so many people interested. The best part of all, was that the bakery box was empty when the day was over.

TREY and his team settled in for the night, he was so damn tired, he just needed to sleep. But first, he wanted to text his family just to let them know he was fine. They had hit a spot with good reception, so he didn't want to miss the opportunity. Once all the family had put their two cents in, his battery was getting low. Fortunately, they were sleeping in, or in *his* case near, their transport vehicle, the *Cat Box*, so he could charge his phone. As he plugged it into one of the chargers he frowned. He'd never heard back from Mary Ann after he sent her the fire picture he'd snapped, when they hit the patch of fire, that had taken them the whole damn day to get out.

He typed out a final message to Mary Ann.

Trey: Fire defeated, Fighting Jaguars – 1, Fire – 10,000,000

Trey: Sweet dreams to a sweet lady.

He left his phone and hit his bed roll, he was asleep before he could wonder why he hadn't heard from her.

MARY ANN LOOKED at the texts she'd gotten from Trey again. *Why is he being so sweet if he's such a douche, although there is something to be said for him not being a dog and hooking up with any woman available.* She shook her head, he hadn't acted like he was too good for her. Yes, he had withdrawn some and left to get some sleep, but he didn't act like she was beneath him. In fact, she was certain he'd been into her on the dance floor. And now he was texting her, often. Talk about mixed messages.

She couldn't bring herself to ignore him a second time. She typed out several replies and then deleted them and tried again. Finally, she texted him back.

Mary Ann: Good luck with the fires, be careful.

There that was perfect, not ignoring him. but not flirty either. Maybe if he kept texting her she could respond with what was going on at the gallery. That would be a good compromise. In fact, she would start that tonight. She brought his name up again and texted.

Mary Ann: Lots of interest in the gallery today, phone is going to melt down soon from all the calls.

She put a little flame emoji at the end and closed the app. Now she needed sleep, because if tomorrow was as crazy as today had been, she needed to be on top of her game. And she'd better charge her phone, because all those calls had drained her battery.

In the morning, there was another text from Trey saying they were leaving Kristen's to return to the fire and he would text when he could. He'd sent her an ice-cube and a phone and a four-leaf clover for luck dealing with all the people calling.

They continued to text back and forth for the next few weeks. Some days she wouldn't get any texts and then she would get a flood of them, so she assumed it was from him being in and out of range of the cell towers. It was fun, and she slowly softened toward him.

When Nolan's mother, Lucille, flew into town and offered to help, Mary Ann was thrilled and a little awestruck. Lucille was a wonderful woman and very down to earth for such a famous artist. Mary Ann enjoyed working with her and between the two of them the gallery was starting to take shape.

Lucille told her all about the pieces she was planning to have shipped for the gallery and she'd even shown her pictures of several of them. It was so exciting.

They spent their days collecting items, pricing them and arranging things. Some artists brought a lot of product and they had to store some of it for future sales. Some didn't bring enough, and Mary Ann asked them if they had more they could bring in.

Kristen walked in one afternoon with some of her own work. "Doesn't this look awesome? You guys are doing a great job. It looks very professional but also cozy, so many galleries have a stiff, formal feel. I sometimes feel nervous wandering through them, but you've hit just the right note of comfort."

Mary Ann was thrilled at the compliment. She and Lucille had talked about making it a friendly environment, like the town was, rather than a formal gallery that wouldn't fit in as well.

Kristen held out her hands filled with jewelry. "Here are some things of mine to add to the collection. I'll try to get a few more items ready, I noticed there were some unfinished projects in the safe that I had started for people and then the commissions fell through. So those won't take a lot of time to get completed. Especially if you can help with the polishing, Mary Ann."

"I'd be happy to." Mary Ann grinned.

Lucille asked, "Could you teach me to help? I think it would be fun to work in a different medium for a while, even if it's just the cleanup. It never hurts to try new things."

Kristen shook her head. "I can't imagine someone as talented as you would want to do cleanup work."

"I think it would be fun."

"Fine with me. I can show you, or Mary Ann can. We have some charms Mary Ann works on." Kristen looked at her. "Maybe we should setup a small work area over here, so that while you keep an eye on the gallery, you can also be working on the charms when it's slow."

Mary Ann nodded. "There is that area off to the side that might be perfect for that. It has good natural light and a view of the showroom."

"Okay, let's do that, we just need to get the buffer over here from your house and we could set up a little workstation. We'd need to set up a plastic enclosure, to keep the buffing medium from getting all over everything. But that shouldn't be too hard."

Lucille spoke up, "I'm sure we could get Nolan to help move whatever needs to be brought over. He is freakishly strong."

Mary Ann smiled and went back to work as Kristen and Lucille went on to talk about taking the dog for a walk. When they finished, she said, "If we're done for the day I'm going to head out. I might have a date with a hotshot, he called and told me he has the weekend off."

Kristen nodded. "Remember what we talked about, and I'll see you Monday."

Mary Ann laughed. "I just might follow your advice."

$\mathcal{T}$rey wasn't sure he should have called Mary Ann to meet him tonight, but he just couldn't keep the darn woman out of his mind. He'd spent the whole three weeks since he'd seen her last, thinking about holding her as they danced and what a fool he'd been not to kiss her. Or at least hang out a while longer, what a chicken-shit he'd been running out on her like he had. He was damn surprised today when she'd sounded excited to meet him.

Fortunately, he'd have some other guys with him, so it wouldn't just be the two of them. He still didn't think he should get involved with a local woman. Who knew when he'd be called to go somewhere else. And of course, at the end of fire season he would be heading back to his home state. So, it was a temporary arrangement at best. Not that he couldn't work from anywhere as a web developer, but he was still planning to leave.

Kevin called out, "Trey, let's get a move on, we're burning daylight and we only have two days off. Move your ass, buddy. There's a cold brew with my name on it and it's nearly an hour down the mountain, on this goat trail they call a road."

"Yeah, yeah don't get your panties in a twist, I'm coming." He walked to the door of Kristen's house to meet up with the team going down for a couple of days.

Kevin whistled. "Well don't you look pretty. I had no idea you could clean up so well, just what is the occasion?"

Trey shook his head. "I shaved and put on clothes that I don't wear to fight fires."

Kevin sniffed. "And aftershave. You got a little honey lined up down there?"

"No. Well I did call Mary Ann, you know the one that was here when we helped evacuate, not the woman who lived here, but her friend."

"Really? She's a cutie. How'd you get her number?"

Trey frowned but nodded. "When Stone got injured I bumped into her by the clinic, we had a brew and a pizza. So, I called her today to say we were coming into town, if she wanted to have a beer with us."

Kevin grinned. "Well maybe I should have shaved and dressed up, too. She might like me better."

"Knock it off, asshole. We're only here a short time." He socked Kevin in the shoulder.

"Yeah, but she might like a little hook up while we are here, you never know about women. If you've got dibs on her maybe she has friends."

"I don't have dibs, dammit." She wasn't a toy for God's sake.

Kevin grinned. "Awesome."

He didn't have dibs, but he didn't want Kevin going after her either. Kevin was starting to piss him off with his attitude. "But keep your hands to yourself."

"Right, not dibs, uh huh, sure, I believe that. Better work on convincing yourself."

Quinn poked his head in the door. "Quit your jawin' and let's move ladies, I've got a powerful thirst going." He looked Trey up and down. "Well now, don't you look pretty."

Kevin laughed, and Trey swore, as they all crammed into the SUV to take them down the mountain.

~

MARY ANN WALKED into Greg's bar and spotted the firefighters right away. Trey had his back to the door and Theresa was bent over him practically shoving her cleavage in his face. Nope, this was not happening. That was her hotshot, and she wasn't sharing, thank you very much. Guess it was time to stake her claim.

Mary Ann walked over and cooed, "Trey darling, there you are, sorry I was late." She pushed between Theresa and her man, grabbed his face and kissed him like there was no tomorrow. At first, he was a little hesitant, probably from shock at her forwardness, but after just a few seconds he got right on board and kissed her back with passion.

The kiss was so hot and delicious that she almost didn't hear Theresa say, "How rude," and flounce off.

Trey kissed her another minute or two, then pulled back and grinned. "Thanks for saving me."

"Not saving you so much as staking a claim, but you're welcome."

"Staking a claim? I think I like that. Would you like to stake your claim out on the dance floor?"

"Yes, I would." She dropped her purse on the table where the rest of the firefighters were sitting in open mouthed astonishment at her audacity. She looked at them, shrugged and said, "You snooze, you lose."

They burst out laughing and Trey pulled her out on the floor. He drew her close and she could feel his strong

48

muscular body fitting very well with her softer one. The song was a fast ballad; the perfect 'get to know you better' dance with a handsome man. Trey was handsome, and he smelled good too, like outdoors, fresh air, and man, with a very faint hint of aftershave and wood smoke. Trey held her close and twirled her around the dance floor. He felt so darn good against her that she'd have been happy to stay like this for a week, maybe two.

After a few minutes of perfection, he asked her, "So about this claim you're staking, may I assume you're single and available?"

"Yes, and I really, really hope you are too."

He smiled a warm smile. "Yes, I am, and I've been thinking for weeks, that you were about the prettiest thing I'd seen in a long time."

"Then why didn't you make a move?"

His smile faded. "I try not to get involved with the locals when we're on assignment. I don't know when we'll be moving on to the next location and I don't want to hurt anyone when I have to leave quickly. I've never been tempted to change that philosophy, until I saw you up on that mountain, trying your best to save our asses from being blown to kingdom come."

"You know, you could just lay the whole issue on the table and let the woman, that would be me, decide if she wants to be with you, if only for a short time."

"Yeah? And what do you think that woman would want, since it *is* you."

"I think she'd want to be with you for any time she can get." She looked him in the eye, "Life is short, and I don't want to always play it safe. That safe road can also be the road to regrets that last a lifetime."

"You're right, and every time I think about you and force myself to back off, it feels like regret."

49

That's a better answer. She grinned at him. "Then let's live life to the fullest and enjoy each other in the time we do have. Plus, I am not some fragile flower that is going to die when you leave."

"Alright you've talked me into it. What do you have in mind?"

She raised an eyebrow in speculation. "How long is your break?"

"We have to be back on the mountain Monday morning at nine."

Two days, she would be more than happy to keep the boy busy for two days. Her girl parts fluttered at that idea. "That gives us the whole weekend. So, we can stay here, have a few more dances and a couple of drinks, chat it up with your friends for an hour or two and then go back to my house and have sex, non-stop, until Monday morning at eight."

Trey's eyes heated. "That sounds like a perfect plan, but we might have to stop by a drugstore on the way for supplies."

She patted his cheek. "Don't you worry your pretty little head about that. I ordered a giant economy sized box of supplies from an online sex toys store. I think we'll be good, maybe for two weekends."

Trey laughed. "Good to know, just like a boy scout, always prepared."

"In this case, it was wishful thinking."

"Your wish is my command."

CHAPTER 9

$\mathcal{M}$ary Ann couldn't believe she'd just propositioned the man and had told him to expect a weekend full of sex. What was she thinking? She had no idea, and she couldn't blame it on drinking, she hadn't even ordered a drink yet. Was Trey going to think she was the biggest 'ho' in town? She wasn't, but you couldn't tell by her talk tonight. What the hell had gotten into her? She let out a soft groan at her own behavior.

Trey pulled back a little from their slow dance and looked at her. "What's wrong?"

"Nothing." She ducked her head and tried to get back closer to hide her face against his shoulder. But he held her off.

"Yes, there is, tell me."

She could feel her face getting hotter and hotter. "It's not important, let's just dance."

"Mary Ann."

"Fine. I'm worried you think I'm a slut, coming on to you like that."

Trey laughed, and his eyes sparkled. "That is so far from

what I'm thinking, it's not even in the same galaxy. What I'm thinking about is how I can calm down and not drag you out of here this minute to have my wicked way with you. What I'm thinking is that I want to show you a good time and treat you like the lady you are, and not let you think I'm some horny guy that wants nothing more than sex."

"Really?"

"Yes, I haven't known you long and I want to take it slow. I want to get to know you better before we jump in the sack. My mind wants that, my body on the other hand is so enthralled with you I hardly know my own name. There is no blood left in the upper portion of my anatomy."

She laughed.

"So, while I would love to drag you out of here cave man style, I think we need to go back to the table and have a drink, and chat with the guys and slow this down a little bit."

"The anticipation might kill us."

He shook his head. "Not kill us, but teach us patience and restraint, yeah it will do that."

"Well then let's go back to the table and work on that, shall we. Maybe we should stick to the fast dances."

He nodded and took her hand to walk back to their table. They ordered some drinks. She ordered a frozen margarita thinking all that ice might help her cool down. Getting back with the other guys helped a lot

All the hotshots tried to impress her with their stories, but she had a few of her own that had them howling with laughter. She and Trey danced a few more times to fast songs and hurried back to the table when the slow ballads came on. One by one the single guys drifted off as they found a lady of their own to enjoy. The married guys went to the game room, to play pool or darts.

Finally, when she could not stand the tension any longer she looked him in the eye. "Enough patience."

TREY SIGHED WITH RELIEF. "Amen to that, my restraint was slipping."

She giggled, and the sound went through him and set every nerve on alert. He threw some money on the table to pay for the last of their drinks that were both still nearly full and they hurried out the door. Fortunately, most of the other hotshots were busy when they left, so they didn't generate too much attention, but a few comments were made.

Enough that Trey knew the guys would razz him on Monday. But he frankly didn't care if they did. He was going home with the prettiest girl in the place and she was excellent company too. He'd had more fun with her in the two evenings he'd spent with her than most people he'd known for years.

It was a great night; the heat of the day had dissipated with the cool breeze blowing in from the lake. Outside the bar, in the quiet, it was peaceful, and they could talk without shouting.

"I didn't drive, but I don't live far. I was planning to walk back."

"I'm happy to escort you and be your protection."

She nudged his shoulder. "I don't really need protection; this is a very safe town. We've never had any need to worry about being out at night alone. But I have plans for you, so you better come with me."

"Oh, well in that case, maybe we should walk faster."

"No can do, I wore sexy shoes tonight and my feet hurt, so we'll just have to go slow." She screeched as he swept her up in his arms and carried her quickly down the street. "Put me down. I'm too heavy to carry."

He laughed. "You met the guys in there tonight, I can carry every one of them for five miles with both our gear.

You have to have strength and endurance when out fighting a wildland fire."

"All of them? Even that really big guy?"

"Even him, so carrying you is a piece of cake. Or maybe I should say a small bag of feathers."

She grinned and pointed out the next turn they needed to take. When they got to her house, she squirmed. "You need to put me down, so you can open the gate."

"No need." He whipped her up and over his shoulder in a fireman's carry and opened the gate. She laughed and kicked her feet.

He swatted her lightly on the butt. "Now stop that, I don't want to drop you."

He carried her up the steps to the front door and stooped so he could put her down, so she could unlock it. From behind he heard her say, "It's not locked."

"Seriously, that's kind of dangerous, leaving your house unlocked."

"No, I told you it's a safe town."

"But with the influx of tourists you don't have just the locals here anymore, you should start locking your doors." He slipped the bright red sky-high heels off and bent down to put her bare feet on the floor. As he stood he slowly ran his hands up her sides from feet to shoulders. "There you are. Safe and sound and your feet didn't have to walk so far. These don't look very comfortable, but they did make your legs look about two miles long."

"Then they accomplished their goal, and my feet thank you." She put her arms around his neck. "Now are you ever going to kiss me? It's your turn."

"I didn't know we were taking turns, but I am not going to argue about a chance to taste those lips again." He looked at her mouth and felt desire rush through him, he slowly lowered his head and supped, softly tasting, drinking her in

54

gently. Until she reached up and grabbed two handfuls of hair and dragged him down and into the heat. He was lost, she tasted like sin and strawberry margarita, she licked his lips, and he opened his mouth to hers and they plundered each other.

"Bedroom, down the hall." She gasped when they came up for air.

"Right." He bent down, and she was back over his shoulder as he moved like lightning to her room.

She laughed when he tossed her onto the bed. He joined her on top of the quilt and took her chin in his hand while he claimed her mouth. He just couldn't get enough of that mouth. He was fairly certain he could spend the whole weekend just kissing her, drinking her in.

Mary Ann clearly had other plans, however. Her busy hands already had his shirt untucked and unbuttoned, she started stroking his chest and his back. She even ran one hand down the back of his pants and squeezed his ass. With the two brain cells that were still functioning he decided he better pick up his game if he didn't want to disappoint this woman.

Trey rolled them a bit until they were on their sides, so he could find the zipper at the back of her dress. He clasped the tab and started tugging it down, when it was fully unzipped he let his fingers wander over the warm soft skin of her back. Touching that warm silk with just his fingertips, so lightly, she squirmed.

He grinned. "Ticklish?"

"No, I refuse to be ticklish."

"Refuse huh? Then that means you really are but actively fight it." He ran his fingertips up her back.

She shivered and then smacked him. "Stop, you're ruining the mood."

He chuckled. "Uh huh, whatever you say." But he changed

his tickling caress to a firmer one as he ran his hand down her back, under the dress and squeezed her butt, pulling her hips up against his, so she could feel his erection. At the same time, he took possession of her mouth again, plundering and dueling with her tongue.

She put one leg over his hip, bringing her heat closer to his cock, which throbbed behind the fly of his jeans. It was getting painful down there with her pressing up against him and causing more blood to flow south in his body.

He rolled her to her back and she put her legs around his hips. He ground against her as she held onto his ass with both hands, pulling him in even tighter. Rocking against her, he could feel her getting close to release, as her arms and legs held him even tighter. His movement didn't falter, he would have loved to caress her breasts, but you couldn't fit a piece of paper between them and she was still fully dressed in front, so that would have to wait.

She grabbed his hair with one hand and dragged his mouth back to hers, where she pulled his tongue into her mouth and sucked on it. When he reciprocated sucking on her tongue, she blasted off, digging her fingernails into his back with one hand and pulling his hair with the other. What a wildcat she was. He loved it.

After a few minutes, she moaned and said, "Hot." And started pushing him off of her.

He laughed and rolled off, so she could move easily. Then he watched in awe, as she tore her clothes off flinging them across the room. When she had only her panties left on she flopped back on the bed and breathed a sigh of relief. He just grinned at her while his eyes feasted on her body.

She opened one eye and scowled at him. "What are you doing way over there and why are you still dressed?"

"Just admiring the view."

"Well stop admiring the view and get in the picture, preferably naked."

"Yes ma'am." As he shucked off his clothes her other eye opened and then she raised up on her elbows and finally sat all the way up.

When he was fully naked she was busy ogling his body. He stopped moving and just looked at her.

She smiled a sly sexy smile, reached out her hands and said, "Gimme."

Laughing, he stalked toward her.

CHAPTER 10

*M*ary Ann shivered as she watched Trey take off his clothes. The man was built, she'd had her hands on his back and chest, but as he took his shirt all the way off and then started working on his pants she could feel herself practically drooling. He had the perfect male body, wide shoulders, sculpted pecs and abs, with narrow hips. When he pushed his jeans down she could see thick strong thighs and calves. Until he stood back up and his erection stood out proudly from his body, and that did make her mouth water.

He waited patiently for her to look her fill and then chuckled when she'd urged him back to her. When he got close enough she reached out for his cock, it was hard as steel, smooth as velvet, long and thick, and she got wetter just thinking about him inside her.

She hadn't been with a man in longer than she wanted to admit, even to herself, so she had every intention of enjoying herself to the fullest. He wouldn't be in the area long, so she was going to revel in every minute she did have. This was a summer fling, plain and simple. With no strings or demands for the future. She had never done anything like this, she had only ever had sex inside a monogamous long-term relationship. But this was a hookup, nothing more and it felt freeing, she didn't have to worry about what he would think of her in a few months. In a few months, he would be gone. Most likely never to return again, so she was determined to let herself indulge. Wild sex and maybe even some fantasies were the order of the day. This was going to be a weekend that would make her smile when she turned eighty. And if it felt just a little scary to be so wild, she was just going to shove those feelings down deep, this was a once in a lifetime opportunity and she was going to enjoy every second of it.

She stroked his cock and it jumped in her hand, she smiled and stroked it again, this time engaging her other hand in fondling his balls. He let her play for a minute or two before he groaned and said, "If you keep that up much longer it's going to be over before we get started."

She laughed and squeezed him with both hands and then turned him loose to reach into her bedside table to pull out the box of condoms she had ordered. It really was a giant economy size and Trey's eyes widened when he looked at it.

"Damn girl, that is more than a weekend or two."

She grinned. "Challenge accepted." She got the box open and took out a generous handful and set them on the table, keeping one in her hand. With a wicked look, she said, "Those should last us tonight," and put the box back in the drawer.

Trey said in a strangled voice, "Dear God woman, are you trying to kill me?"

"Nope but you might get a work out, I expect to put that hotshot stamina to the test." Then she laughed like crazy at his expression which was a combination of lust and fear. She opened the condom packet and rolled it on him in a slow, purposeful manner, making sure to continue the torture as long as possible. When it was finally on he growled, drew her up fully on the bed, and brought his magnificent body down on top of hers.

She reveled in his weight and spread her legs in invitation. He rested between them, but didn't enter her, instead he started in on her breasts, gently squeezing them, pinching her nipples. Then he took one in his mouth and suckled. She squirmed beneath him and he chuckled and moved to the other breast.

The sensations were exquisite, but she needed more, she wanted him inside her, filling her. "Trey."

He bit down lightly on the nipple in his mouth. Then lifted his head so her breast made a popping sound as it left his mouth and fire shot through her.

"Yes?" he asked innocently.

"Play time is over. I want more."

He grinned. "Just returning the favor. Making sure you're good and ready."

"Inside, now."

"Yes ma'am." Then he thrust inside her and filled her to capacity. Her body stretched and made room for his inhabitation. It was glorious. She wrapped her legs around his hips and locked her ankles together to keep him right where she wanted him. Not that he was going anywhere, as he set up a pattern of long smooth strokes that would drive her wild and she loved it. Each thrust drew her higher and higher until she felt she was no longer on earth, but on a plane high above it, and when she shattered she knew some of her drifted away to float in space for all time. She felt like Trey was floating out there with her.

It took her a long time to regain a consciousness of where she was. In her own home in her own bed with a man that was apparently a sex god. She had never had anything like that happen before, so he clearly must have some special skills.

Trey rolled off of her and lay gasping. "Wow that was unreal. I feel like I just came apart into nothing, like I was caught in a transporter and disintegrated for a moment. Although I'm not sure all the pieces came back. Girl, you pack a powerful punch."

"I was kind of thinking along those same lines, although I didn't relate it to a transporter."

"Sorry. I'm kind of a geek and I've always wondered how it would feel to be transported molecule by molecule. I think I've got a handle on it now."

Mary Ann giggled. "Well don't tell anybody, but I'm a bit of a science fiction freak too. Maybe if you're good, I'll let you see my collection."

He growled. "Oh, I can be good alright, are you ready for round two yet?"

"Maybe."

"I'll be right back, need to dispose of round one." She pointed the way to the bathroom and he left to go take care of things.

She happily watched his magnificent naked form walk across the room to the door. As he turned to go out of it she saw huge scratches on his back and gasped. Had she scratched the hell out of his back? No, she couldn't have, she'd never done anything like that before. This had been a completely different experience, but still.

WHEN TREY WALKED BACK in the bedroom Mary Ann was sitting up with the sheet over her, and she was nearly as pale as the sheet. He hurried over to the bed.

"Mary Ann what's wrong?"

She looked like she was going to throw up. "I scratched you, your back, it's all scratched up. How could I be so vicious?"

He chuckled and pulled her close. "I would expect nothing less from my little wildcat, you don't see me complaining."

"But…"

"No, now stop. It's only a few little scratches, you didn't break the skin. I'm sure they're already fading." He pulled away and turned his back toward her. "Am I right?"

She let out a huge sigh. "Yes, they are fading, but still. I didn't know I was doing it, you should have stopped me."

"There was no way I had any capacity to stop anything." He laughed. "I was right there in oblivion with you."

"Well I'm not doing that again, I'll just lay on my hands or something. I don't want you going back all scratched up and bloody from being with me. It might attract bears."

Wasn't she cute, all worried about him and bears. They saw bears all the time, usually moving the opposite direction they were going. The bears away from the fire, while their team moved toward it. He took her hand and looked at it. "Now don't be silly you have short trimmed nails that aren't going to cause me any harm. If you had some of those long stiletto type nails, some women have, I might be scared, but these are no threat." He rubbed a thumb over her finger tips.

"Oh, I keep them short to work on the jewelry. I had them longer, but they kept getting in my way and catching on things. So, I cut them off."

"See. Now I have nothing to worry about and I kind of liked you going all wildcat on me. You know, all this talk about round two is giving me ideas. In fact, you can be on top this time, so no back to scratch. Deal?"

"Oh, I like the sound of that. You've got yourself a deal."

He pulled the sheet from her and down to the foot of the

bed then laid down smack dab in the middle of the mattress with his arms and legs outstretched. "I'm all yours."

She rubbed her hands together and leered at him. "Now where to start?"

Trey woke up the next morning with his little wildcat wrapped around him like cellophane, and he didn't mind it one bit. She was laying half on top of him with her head on his chest, nearly beneath his chin. One hand was wrapped around his waist and the other under his shoulder. One leg was between his with her foot wrapped around his leg. Normally he wasn't much of a cuddler, he liked his space when he slept. He didn't have many sleep-overs with women, he generally spent a few hours with a woman and then went home to his own house to sleep.

He'd only had one live-in girlfriend, and she had liked her space too, so they'd had a king-sized bed where they both had plenty of room. Sometimes the Fighting Jaguars all had to sleep like sardines in the *Cat Box*, if it wasn't safe or good enough weather for some of them to sleep outside. Trey didn't like sleeping cramped in the *Cat Box,* so he was almost always out camping under the stars or in many cases the smoky haze.

He was surprised to find himself quite content with Mary Ann wrapped around him. They had indulged in each other a lot last night, learning how to please the other. What touch and taste felt best, what reaction each caress evoked. They had experimented and adjusted and learned the other's body, over and over, until they had finally passed out from sheer exhaustion.

But now with her breasts pressed into his chest and her hot center on one of his legs he felt his body start to wake up. He couldn't move without disturbing her, but he didn't want to wake her up with a boner poking into her, either. Maybe he could think about something else. Nope, his mind was fully centered on the delectable bit of woman in his arms. Especially when she squirmed on top of him, every nerve stood on alert as did another part of him.

She squirmed again and then without opening her eyes reached down and took hold of that part of his anatomy that was on high alert. She didn't push it to the side like he thought she would, since it was poking into her. Oh no, she was fondling it, making him harder by the second.

When Trey groaned, she looked up at him lazily through her lashes and gave him a sleepy smile. "Ready to go again, I see."

"You are wrapped around me, how else am I going to react to your soft skin and delightful curves."

She grinned at him with a predatory smile. "Exactly as you have."

The rest of the weekend was spent doing four things, sleeping, eating, having sex, and watching episode after episode of Mary Ann's science fiction collection. They both loved the classic versions of Star Trek and Battle Star Galactica. The dent they put into watching all of her collection was tiny, because other appetites kept intruding, but neither one of them were complaining, they could always watch TV and movies anytime.

CHAPTER 11

*M*onday morning Trey managed to drag himself to the rendezvous point, to return up the mountain. He was exhausted, and that was hard to accomplish with a hotshot, they were trained in all kinds of physical challenges, including sleep deprivation. Not that he was truly sleep deprived, he and Mary Ann had spent a lot of time sleeping, it's just that they had also spent a lot more time doing the horizontal tango. And when they weren't horizontal they had enjoyed each other on every surface in the house.

He got in the vehicle and announced they needed to stop by the florist. Before the smartasses in the transport could comment he said, "The Fighting Jaguars are going to send Kristin and Mary Ann flowers for the art gallery grand opening. It's the least we can do."

The guys nodded, acknowledging that it was a huge luxury to have a house as a base of operations for the summer. He dragged into the florist and asked her to send a large bouquet on opening day and used the hundred-dollar bill that he kept as emergency cash in his wallet.

Trey hardly looked at his team mates when he climbed into the transport, curled up and passed out for the entire drive up the mountain. When he awoke, the whole base crew was crowded around the vehicle grinning at him. He scowled back.

"So, sleeping beauty. I take it the wild woman used you up and spit you out." Kevin raised his eyebrow, daring him to deny it.

There was no use doing that, they had all seen him leave with her and not join them the rest of the time they were in town. They had even texted him a couple of times to let him know where he could join them, if he was so inclined. He'd ignored those texts and wished he could have turned off his phone.

He shrugged, "Jealous, Kevin?"

"Hell yes, I'm jealous. Mary Ann is one fine-looking woman, and she sank her claws into you the minute she walked in the door."

"Yes, she did, and it was amazing. Now don't we have a fire to fight?"

"Not today. The Super said we would go out tomorrow, stay out until we get the fire break completed, we'll have a briefing in a couple of hours."

Trey grinned. "Excellent, I'm going to get my pack ready for tomorrow, before the briefing, and then I can hit the hay early tonight."

"Want to work out later?" Kevin asked.

"God no, believe me I had plenty of exercise this weekend. I need food and sleep. That's it."

Keven just laughed at him, and Trey smirked back.

MARY ANN WALKED into the shop, and knew she was glowing, she couldn't help herself it had been an exceptional weekend.

Kristen took one look at her and demanded. "Oh, my God, you got laid, didn't you?"

"Yes, I did, all weekend, and it was glorious."

"All weekend?"

"All. Weekend. Friday night. Saturday. Sunday. All. Weekend."

"I assume my advice worked then."

"Like a charm. When I walked into the bar and saw Theresa all up in his grill shoving her enormous tits in his face, I had no choice but to stake my claim. So, I stepped right in between her and my hotshot and kissed the stuffing out of him."

Kristen was looking at her in awe. "Right there in the middle of the bar? In front of God and everybody?"

"Yes, I did. Theresa stomped off in a snit and the rest of the hotshots were shocked as hell. I just said something snarky and they all laughed. We went out on the dance floor and I invited the man back to my house for a weekend of sex. He didn't turn me down."

"Well the guy isn't stupid."

Mary Ann ducked her head. "I kind of felt like a slut after that and wondered if he would think I was a big 'ho'."

Kristen put her hands on her hips and frowned. "Well if he treated you like…"

"No, he didn't he was very sweet and treated me like a lady. But you have to admit it was rather forward of me. I've only seen the guy a couple of times and we've done some texting back and forth."

"Don't you worry about it, everyone is entitled to at least one summer fling in their life. And who knows when he'll be called away so…" Kristen shrugged.

"Yeah, that's kind of what I told him. When he said he

didn't normally get involved with local girls when he's on a hotshot assignment. That you only live once and who wants regrets to fill their memories."

"Wow, that is pretty profound."

"I don't know if it's profound, but it's not the way I want to live my life. Being tied to this tiny town is bad enough. I've always dreamed of seeing the world, but it's not really a practical dream." Mary Ann stuffed her longing for adventure down, it wasn't happening any time soon. Thinking of how much fun she was having working with Kristen, on a daily basis, went a long way to soothing that ache.

She grinned at Kristen. "So, what are you going to teach me today? I love working with you by the way, so don't think you're getting rid of me any time soon."

"Well I was actually going to have you try making one of my most popular earring designs all by yourself. Then turn you free to do some innovations of your own."

Kristen showed Mary Ann an earring design she wanted her to work on. Mary Ann was beside herself with excitement about creating her very own jewelry, yes it was one of Kristen's designs, but she could put her own little touches on it. She did the first one exactly the same as Kristen's, just to make sure she knew what she was doing.

"Here is my first pair, what do you think?" She asked nervously.

Kristen took them in her hand and turned them over, she looked at the post that was soldered on the back and the design touches on the front. Kristen yanked on the pearl that dangled in the center of the moon shape and it stayed secure. She held them both up by the posts and looked at them, probably to see if they hung straight, they did.

Finally, she nodded. "Excellent work, Mary Ann. Now to complete the piece, stamp a little number one on the back, and from now on number anything you make."

Mary Ann felt like she'd won the lottery, she'd gotten everything right. Her smile was huge and when she clapped her hands in glee, Kristen just laughed.

"Goody, I'm going to start on another pair." An idea had popped in her head about a little different design for the front of the next pair. She wanted to put a little border of etches all around it and leave the center a little plainer. If Kristen hated it maybe she would buy it for herself.

She vaguely heard the house and gallery doorbell ring. After a few seconds she looked up, Kristen smiled at her. "I'll get it, you go ahead and keep working."

"Thanks." She grinned and went back to working on the earrings. When Kristen didn't come back Mary Ann started to wonder if something was wrong. There was only one step left in the process to finish the set of earrings, but warning bells were going off in her head, so she put down her work and hustled toward the gallery.

When she got in the door she saw Kristen standing in the middle of the room surrounded by boxes, all the color had drained from her face and she looked like she might faint. "You didn't come back, what's wrong? You look like you've seen a ghost."

Kristen looked up with a dazed expression. "Not a ghost, just a million dollars in art."

A million dollars? It must be Lucille's work. She'd told Mary Ann all about each piece she was sending, how to unpack them and how best to display each piece. She clapped her hands, "Oh goody, Lucille's art came. Let's open it."

Kristen shouted, "Oh hell no! We are not going to open it, not until Nolan or Lucille or preferably both are here. You knew she was sending a million dollars of art?"

"Yes of course, she told me all about the pieces she was sending."

"But a million dollars…"

Mary Ann shrugged, that wasn't really much money for Lucille's art. Mary Ann had studied her in school and knew sometimes one piece would go for a million, so six pieces seemed like a bargain. Then again, she knew Kristen's family had been pretty poor, after her father had run off with a younger woman and left his family to fend for themselves. It had been quite the town gossip for a while when she was a kid. Enough so that she remembered it, and she hadn't been very old at the time. Mary Ann on the other hand had grown up in a slightly above middle-class family, where her father had a good job and her mother had a small home-based business, so the prices didn't seem so high to her. "What did you think she was going to send?"

"I don't know, but I didn't think it would be that much. That's like a hundred and fifty thousand each." Kristen huffed.

"Yes, it is, and her art is worth every penny."

"But who will buy it?"

What a stupid question. This was *Lucille Thompson's* work, they were going to have people beating down the doors to buy it. She snorted. "Oh, you just get the word out that you have her art in your little gallery here, and you'll have plenty of people coming to buy it. Tourist problems are going to be a thing of the past, my friend. In fact, you better get some high-end jewelry ready for those rich people to buy. That three-thousand-dollar pendant of yours will be a drop in the bucket."

Kristen sank down, right on the floor, in the middle of the showroom. "I don't think I can handle this."

Oh dear, poor Kristen was a mess, Mary Ann sat next to her and took one of her cold hands and started rubbing it to bring the warmth back. "It will be just fine, don't worry."

Kristen laid down on the floor and laughed a little hysterically. "Right. Just fine."

Oh dear, what should she do now? Just let Kristen lay in the middle of the floor? Should she call someone? Do something? Maybe distraction would work. "You know I'm almost done with the second set of earrings and I did something a little different with them. I only have to put the pearl on and they'll be done. But I wanted you to see the design and see if it was okay."

"Yeah, I can do that."

"Good can we go over and look at them now? It's getting kind of late. And didn't you say Nolan was coming to my house this afternoon, when he gets off work, to bring the buffer so we can set up my mini workspace?"

"Yes, he is. So, let's go look at your creations, that's a better idea than me laying here all worried about the art."

CHAPTER 12

*L*ater that afternoon, Mary Ann answered the knock on her door to see Nolan. "So how is Kristen? Is she still freaked out?"

"She's not laying in the middle of the showroom floor anymore, so that must mean she's better." Mary Ann watched his reaction to the idea of Kristen laying in the middle of the floor, it was quite comical. "She grew up pretty poor, so I think the idea of that much money is over-whelming."

"Let's get this stuff loaded, so we can get over there. Mom is going to meet us in a half hour or so."

"Oh goody, an unveiling party." Mary Ann grinned.

Nolan laughed. "Yeah, I guess it is."

They loaded all the equipment and supplies, that Mary Ann had brought to her house to work on the charms, into their cars and drove to the gallery. As they carried it all in, Kristen came down from upstairs and they arranged the work area. The Plexiglas walls had arrived on the ferry and they were set up to surround the work area and keep the buffing compound contained. It was going to be a nice cozy place for Mary Ann to work and also keep her eye on the door for customers.

A few minutes later, as they were just finishing up, Amber walked in carrying something that smelled wonderful. All three of them stopped and sniffed. Then they just left whatever they had been doing or saying and were drawn to the meal. Like those cartoons where the person or animal would float toward the food following the aroma.

Lucille walked in following Amber and they all gathered around to eat some amazing jambalaya that her cook had whipped up. He loved Cajun food and very rarely got to make it since it wasn't a normal Pacific Northwest food. But it smelled wonderful and was delicious. While they stuffed their faces there was no talking, just hard eating. Silence reigned in the room, it was almost eerie.

Mayor Carol bustled in the door. "I heard you got Lucille's art in today, so I wanted to come see."

"Great to have you, Mayor," Kristen said graciously.

Kyle and Samantha came in a few minutes later. Kyle said, "Hey, we came to see the show. And Samantha brought pie for after."

Barbara, Chris, Greg and Terry came in next. Followed by Jeremy.

Kristen looked like she was going to throw up the delicious dinner they had just finished, as all her friends and neighbors came in the door. And then Gus came in with his camera.

"Howdy folks, thought we should run a little article about bagging one of the world's most famous artist's work, to be sold in our little town. Gonna put some pictures in the brochure, too."

That statement made all the blood drain from Kristen's face.

"And ya should put up a website to advertise. With Mrs.

Thompson's work you'll draw in tourists with big money. Good thinking, Kristen."

Lucille beamed. "Please call me Lucille, Gus, and I do hope you're right and my art is a draw for people to come and enjoy your town. Let's get them opened, shall we? Nolan, you know how they're packed. Will you do the honors?"

"Of course, I brought some tools with me."

Mary Ann could hardly contain her excitement as Nolan started to unpack the boxes. Of course, the art was well secured with packing materials, so it wasn't a fast process. But it was so exciting that no one seemed to notice how long it took.

When Nolan finally got the first piece unpacked everyone oohed and aahed. Lucille looked at her and nodded. Mary Ann was so happy to show Nolan where to put it. She and Lucille had planned out each location. As each piece was unwrapped and set in its place, Mary Ann felt her heart grow larger almost like that movie about Christmas and the Grinch. She was so proud to be a part of what was going to be an amazing art gallery. She just wanted to stand and stare at all the beauty.

But Samantha announced, "Now let's celebrate with pie. I brought cherry and blueberry."

Even Mary Ann couldn't turn down Samantha's pie, so they all pitched in bagging up the packing materials while Samantha dished up the pie. Then as they ate everyone wandered around the building looking at all it had to offer. She watched as each person looked at all the things for sale. She could see interest in their eyes, this place was going to be amazing.

Kristen came up to her. "I had no idea we had wood carvings from Tim Jefferson in our mix."

"Yes, he brought them in and asked if they were good enough to put in the gallery. Lucille was here at the time and we both told him they were excellent. He told us a story about how Ellen had given him his first good adult pocket knife when he was ten years old. At their first Christmas together, before she and Hank got married. He said it was his most prized possession and he'd worn it out with carving."

"That's awesome, we should have Gus write that up for his brochure, that's the kind of stories that draw people."

"He said he has hundreds of carvings. He wanted to sell them for ten dollars each. Lucille told him they were worth way more than that. So, he agreed to let her price them. He didn't even stay to see what price she put on them but said to call him when we need more."

"Really? That is so cool. Gus, come over here, Mary Ann has a story to tell you."

Mary Ann smiled at Gus and told him all about what Tim had told her and Lucille.

He grinned at her. "Any more stories like that I want to hear them. In fact, think back over the last few weeks, and write up any cute stories you think of and email them to me."

"I will do that Gus. This is so exciting, isn't it?"

"It surely is, Mary Ann. Do you know if you're legal to sell yet? That blue and turquoise piece of Lucille's would look very good in my house foyer."

"I don't know, but I can ask Kristen."

On her way over to talk to Kristen, Terry stopped her and asked, "So can we buy stuff tonight?"

"I don't know, Terry. Let me ask Kristen."

She hurried over to Kristen. "So, are we open for business? Several people have asked me if they can buy things."

"Really? Well, I guess so. I think all the paperwork is complete. We have the scanner for credit cards, we could take cash or checks and just put them in a drawer or something."

"Good," she raised her voice, "Kristen says we're legal to sell, so anyone who wants to, can buy things tonight."

Mary Ann nearly clapped her hands in glee as everyone moved toward the items they had their eye on. Just the glass art Gus wanted was two hundred thousand dollars. By the time she took everyone's credit cards, checks and cash the total was a quarter of a million dollars in sales. Their first foray into business was a huge success and that was from just a few locals. And they weren't even open yet!

Lucille came over to her. "I guess I better get some more stock on its way here. I'm going to leave tomorrow, to go back home, I need to work on my new idea."

Gus said to Lucille, "Well it's been grand having you visit our town, so please come back again soon."

"Oh, I will, do not doubt that, after all my son lives here now, you'll be seeing a lot of me."

Mayor Carol gave her a hug. "We're going to hold you to that."

All their friends and neighbors started making their way home with their packages until it was just her, Kristen, and Nolan left. Mary Ann spun in a circle and then grabbed Kristen and spun her too. "Can you believe how much money we made tonight? And we're not even open. Can you imagine what will happen when the word gets out and it's not friends and neighbors? I am so excited."

Kristen smiled. "I hope you're right and it wasn't just a fluke tonight, or everyone feeling obligated to buy something."

"Oh, I don't think it was that at all. I think they all wanted what they wanted, and they didn't like the idea of waiting and allowing someone else to grab what they had their eye on."

Nolan spoke up, "I think Mary Ann is correct, when you said it was okay to open, everyone made a beeline for what had caught their eye earlier. I saw no hemming and hawing, or people trying to find something. In fact, I saw some of them trying to hold back. I think Samantha picked up and put down that fancy clock five times before she bought it."

They chatted about having a grand opening and some ideas for that. Then Nolan asked, "Have you hired any help besides Mary Ann?"

"No, not really. I have a couple of other people who do some of the finishing work for me. I haven't talked to any of them about coming in and manning the gallery. But I need to, Mary Ann and I can't run it seven days a week. I think it should be open from eleven am until about eight pm, that's nine hours. So, we could use maybe two more people, one that wants to work evenings and one or two for weekends. It might be good to have overlap on weekends when we might be busier."

Oh shoot, Mary Ann had forgotten to ask Kristen about Tammy working with them. She fidgeted and shuffled her feet. "I mentioned the gallery to Tammy O'Conner, she said she'd love to work in it on the weekends in the morning, before Jeff goes to Greg's, that way he could watch the little ones. I hope you don't mind me telling her about it."

"Not at all. I think that would be a great idea, she'd also be good for school days during school hours, as backup. Call her tomorrow. Any other suggestions?"

"Not right off the top of my head, but I'll think about it."

"Good, you've been here all day, go home and relax."

She was exhausted from the busy day, so she saluted. "Yes, ma'am." She gathered up her purse to go home and have a nice long soak in the tub.

TREY WAS DOZING when he heard his phone chime with an

incoming text. Since they were going to be out fighting the monster first thing in the morning, he decided he better check his messages when he could. He grinned when he saw it was from Mary Ann.

Mary Ann: OMG you are not going to believe it! Lucille's art came in today and half the town came to see it be unpacked.

Trey: What a surprise. NOT! Everyone seems to know everything in your town.

Mary Ann: LOL You noticed that did you. Anyway, the not going to believe it part is that we sold over $250K and we aren't even open yet!!!

Trey: That's awesome, congrats.

Mary Ann: Thanks, everyone there had their eye on something, so when Kristen said we were legal to sell they snatched it all up.

Trey: You must be very proud.

Mary Ann: Proud but exhausted, so if I fall asleep mid-text, don't worry.

Trey: LOL, you wore me out so bad that I slept all the way back up the mountain this morning and then took a two-hour nap after our briefing.

Mary Ann: And here I was working.

Trey: Yep you are a much stronger person than I am! BTW We'll be going out to fight the monster first thing in the morning, so you might not hear from me much.

Mary Ann: OK, be careful. I'll be thinking about you.

Trey: Yeah in between making awesome sales and getting that place up and running!

Mary Ann: You betcha, as Gus would say.

Trey: LOL I'll be thinking about you too.

Mary Ann: Good, let me know next time you'll be in town.

Trey: Will do, probably a couple of weeks at least.

Mary Ann: Boo But stay safe, don't let any trees whack you or bears snack on you.

Trey: I'll try, sweet dreams lovely lady.

Mary Ann: Hmm maybe I'll dream of you and have hot ones instead.

Trey: LOL, that works. TTYL

Mary Ann: Bye for now.

Trey put his phone down and laid back down to get some sleep, wondering about her hot dreams. She was quite the little firecracker. He'd never known a more passionate woman, and she owned it. She didn't try to hide her feelings, she was right up front about them. It was so refreshing, he knew exactly where he stood with her. She told him what she wanted and then grabbed hold of that with both hands. He was enjoying their summer fling and would be sorry to see it end when the fire season was over, or he was shipped off to a new location. But that was his life.

CHAPTER 13

$\mathcal{T}$he next morning when Mary Ann got to the studio she was still trying to think of who she could get to help in the gallery, she'd made some phone calls last night, but everyone was working. With the amusement park bringing in families on vacation the unemployment in town had dropped to zero. Jobs had opened up in many of the established businesses, the diner, the bakery and of course the amusement park. Even some of the stay at home moms were busy helping Barbara sew costumes.

She'd called Tammy and confirmed with her to help out in the mornings and possibly longer hours once school started back up. She was still wracking her brain when Kristen finally came in. If she hadn't been so distracted trying to find help she might have wondered at her late appearance, but it hadn't even registered. Kristen had given her a key to the studio, so she'd just let herself in and started working on the earrings.

Kristen sat down next to her. Mary Ann finished the solder she was doing and then looked up.

"So, Nolan had a suggestion last night that I thought was

a great idea. Would you be interested in being my partner in the gallery?"

"What? Your partner. Really?" Mary Ann was flabbergasted, she had no more thought about being a partner than flying to the moon. She was flattered by the idea but wasn't sure she was capable of being a partner.

"Yes. You've done most of the work and are the one most interested in it. I think you should have a defined stake in it. Don't you?"

"Well sure, but a partner? Really? I never thought of a partner, maybe the manager or something, but not a partner. I don't have any money to invest."

"There isn't really any money needed. I own the house, everything's already in place. There might be some incidental costs and salaries, but we made enough the night of the glass unveiling to pay for those kinds of things. If you're interested, I'll get my lawyer to draw up an agreement, we can hammer out the details. So, are you interested?"

Thoughts of traveling with Trey and seeing more of the world flit through her mind, but those were only foolish ideas. Trey hadn't invited her to go with him, they hadn't even talked about anything past the summer. This was an excellent opportunity, probably one that would never come her way again. "Well, I would be a fool not to be, and I am no fool. Yes, I'm interested."

Kristen beamed at her. "Excellent. So, my idea is we'll both work in the studio in the mornings and then you can work on the gallery opening in the afternoons. I'll keep working here, unless you need me. Sound good?"

"Yes, I want to keep learning and creating more. With Tammy working once we open I think I'll still have most of the morning, since the ferries don't start arriving until eleven. I just hope I can find us a few more helpers."

"Yeah, I hope you can too. Unless this is a bust, we'll need a few more. But I also want you to continue growing as a designer, then regardless of what happens to the gallery you'll always be able to create. I was thinking you should branch out a bit and start forming some designs of your own."

Mary Ann blushed. "I do have some ideas, I've sketched a few."

"Good, bring them in tomorrow and I can look them over and offer suggestions."

"I will."

~

THE FIGHTING JAGUARS were taking a quick fifteen-minute break to eat their lunch. They'd been working like dogs doing a burn out between the primary control line and the fire. If they could complete a low intensity burn of all the grass and undergrowth, then the probability of ignition would drop drastically. It was harder for the heavy fuels such as trees and timber to ignite without the undergrowth to feed it. It was a great day for doing the burn out with the perfect weather conditions, so they were trying to get as much done as possible before the weather changed.

"Hey, get away from that," Finn, one of the rookies, yelled. "That's mine."

Trey looked toward the commotion and saw a camp robber had hold of a sandwich. Finn had set the sandwich down while he dug a bag of chips and a sports drink out of his pack. Those grey jays were not afraid of people and Trey had seen this one trailing them earlier. The birds knew where people were there was food. So, they often followed by flying from tree to tree watching for snacks. If you really wanted to, you could get them to eat right out of your hand. They would start with a fly by, snatch and grab, if you held out food. But eventually you could lure them to sit right on your arm, or shoulder and feed them.

Finn managed to get part of his sandwich away from the greedy bird, but not all of it. The bird had snagged a nice portion for himself. Trey managed to snap a picture of the tug of war, he thought Mary Ann might like to see it. Wait a minute, Mary Ann? Usually when he snapped a picture, while they were on the job, he sent it to his sisters or his parents, but now the first person he thought of was Mary Ann. His family would get a kick out of it too, but the real question was why he was thinking about Mary Ann first. She was supposed to be a temporary hook up, but now that he was thinking about it, he realized he sent her texts and pictures pretty often. He listened with half an ear to the other guys as they laughed at Finn, while he scrolled through his texts.

Quinn, the team's sawyer, said, "Gotta keep your food in your hand when the camp robbers start following the team, kid."

"I didn't even see him following us," Finn whined. "Stupid bird."

"If the bird is stupid and got half of your sandwich what does that make you?" Kevin asked.

Finn hung his head. "A dumbass. Do you think this other half is safe to eat?"

"Hell, kid you've been living out here in the woods the same as the bird, for the last few weeks, what do you think he's got that you don't?" Quinn asked with a laugh.

"Rabies?"

Trey put his phone away surprised at what he'd discovered and grinned at Finn.

Kevin laughed. "Eat it or not, but make up your mind, you've got about two minutes left before we get back to fighting the monster. Lunch break is nearly over. Let's get a move on, guys."

Everyone quickly turned back to their own lunch and finished up. They were racing the weather, the clock and the fire. There was no time to dilly-dally. Trey hustled with the rest of them while his mind turned over the fact that he had been sending Mary Ann three to four times the number of texts he was sending his family. He wondered what that meant.

CHAPTER 14

*T*he next few days were spent busily working between the studio and the gallery grand opening. Mary Ann thought about Trey now and then and hoped he was safe. In fact, she thought about him more often than she wanted to. He would just leap into her mind and the memories of their weekend together would flare up in a wave of heat and lust.

He'd told her she wouldn't hear from him much for at least two weeks. They didn't have time off too often, but he promised to let her know when he had another few days off. She occasionally got a text or picture from him, but it was rarely a two-way conversation, his cell reception was never great, so just random things came through. Sometimes it would be a flurry of messages that he had obviously sent out over a couple of days. She sent him texts too, knowing he would get them when he could.

In some ways, she was glad he wasn't around while she was getting ready for the grand opening, so she wasn't distracted, although some stress relief would have been good. She was having trouble finding people to work for them, and she felt like she was letting Kristen down. But so many people worked in the amusement park that it wasn't an easy task to find helpers. She had called everyone she could think of, but wasn't having a lot of luck, she still needed someone for evenings and someone for weekend afternoons.

She'd just hung up the phone from talking to Samantha about the cookies she was planning to bring for the grand opening, Mary Ann was going to text her some pictures of a few of the gallery objects, so Samantha could make cookies that resembled them. The phone rang, and she assumed it was Samantha calling her back. "Yes, I missed you too, but it's only been a few seconds."

A man cleared his throat. "Um, is this the gallery?"

"Oh, sorry I thought… well never mind. Yes, this is the gallery how can I help you?"

"This is Tim Jefferson, and I heard you were looking for some evening help. I was wondering if you would consider me."

She was so excited she thought she might pee her pants, but she tried to maintain her dignity. "Well Tim, we are looking for more help, what did you have in mind?"

"I work on the ranch during the day, but I would kind of like to be involved in the art gallery in the evenings. It would have to be after five, we work until then, often later, but I talked to dad and he said he could spare me by four thirty. So, I could shower and get there by five."

"That would probably work. Can you come in for an interview with me and Kristen?"

"I could come in on Tuesday next week, would that work, the grand opening is the following weekend, isn't it?"

"Yes, I think Tuesday would be good. We'll see you that evening." Mary Ann hung up the phone, did a little victory dance, and hurried out to tell Kristen the news.

When she rushed into the studio Kristen startled. "What the hell? Is something wrong?"

"No, sorry, I was just so excited, I had to come tell you. Tim Jefferson called, and asked if he could work evenings!"

"Yay?" Kristen looked confused.

"I have been having so much trouble trying to find someone to work evenings, almost everyone is working at the amusement park now. I felt like doing cartwheels when he called, but instead I calmly asked him to please come in for an interview. He agreed to come in on Tuesday before the grand opening. Isn't that wonderful? He asked if he could come in after five because he has to finish up his day at the ranch. I told him that would be fine, is it okay with you?"

Kristen smiled. "Tuesday is great. I'd like to talk to him about his art too. I think he'd be an asset, if he doesn't have that silent, brooding, cowboy thing going on."

"Yeah that wouldn't work too well in the gallery. I still need someone for weekend evenings."

Kristen said, "I can do that until we find someone. I should probably spend some time in the gallery, at least while we are just getting started."

"It wouldn't be too much?"

"I wouldn't want to do it forever, but a few weeks or a month or two would be okay."

Mary Ann sighed. "If you're certain, that would give me a little more time to look around. And it would let me work on the grand opening more, rather than continuing to wrack my brain and call everyone I can think of."

"Yes, I can do it, for a while."

Mary Ann grinned. "Yay! But right now, I better get back over there." And she charged back out the door.

~

87

THE FIGHTING JAGUARS were following a trail up to the top of a ridge. There was a meadow on the other side, according to their maps, that they needed to assess. To see if they should do a burn out to get rid of the low-lying vegetation. If there wasn't a lot of trees to catch fire they might be able to leave the grass and bushes.

Finn, the rookie on their team asked, "What's that weird sound? It sounds like something screaming in pain."

Quinn shook his head. "I'm guessing you don't hunt, that's a bull elk mating call. There are probably some elk on the other side of this ridge."

"Male elk make that screaming noise? Really? Are you sure about that?"

"It's called bugling. You'll see when we top that ridge, kid."

Trey shook his head as they continued the last few feet of their climb, this was most likely going to be something Finn had never seen before. Since fire season continued into September and October it was fairly common that they would come upon elk in rut.

They got to the top of the hill and below them was a valley with some aspen trees, a small watering hole and a herd of elk. A couple dozen females were in the bull's harem.

Kevin said, "We've got time to watch the show."

"What show?" Finn asked.

Trey chuckled. "Just watch."

They hunkered down and got some snacks and drinks out of their packs, no reason not to hydrate and refuel at the same time.

"Why is that one hitting his antlers on the tree?" Finn asked.

"That's a sign of aggression, that is a younger bull elk challenging the older one for the opportunity to mate with the harem." Quinn explained.

Finn laughed. "Do they really call it a harem?"

"Yep, and the bull is very protective about his females, he will fight to the death if necessary."

Trey remembered his first time coming upon a scene like this. He'd been in awe of the process. It was still a magnificent thing to watch.

The younger bull approached the older one, antlers down. The older bull locked antlers with the younger one and the wrestling match was on. The sound of the antlers clacking against each other filled the air with a rattling sound. The two males pushed back and forth for several minutes.

Finn said, "This is kind of anti-climactic."

Quinn rolled his eyes. "Just wait, patience is a virtue."

The older bull got the younger one's head turned, exposing a shoulder and gouged his antlers into it. Finn gasped as the blood flowed. It looked like the younger bull was going to pursue the fight, but then he stumbled and backed off. The older bull must have recognized the surrender because he lowered his head and resumed eating. The younger bull limped off.

Finn was wide eyed. "That was amazing. Man, that's a hard way to keep a woman. I'm glad I'm a human and not an elk. Why didn't the older one keep fighting? Will the younger one come back again? Does this happen a lot? What happens if it's the older one that gets hurt, does he stop like the younger one did or fight to the death? Will the hurt one be okay, should we try to help it?"

Kevin frowned. "It's nature, we don't know all the answers except one. Those are wild animals, you don't *help* them. They weigh seven hundred pounds or more. He's hurt and pissed off, *you* don't go near them. Ever."

"I won't," Finn promised.

"Good, I think we'll leave the elk alone in that valley for now, let's cut to the north and see what it looks like on the other side of the valley. If we can keep the fire from getting close, we might be able to let these animals stay here safely."

Kevin started moving north along the ridgeline. Trey brought up the rear and thought about what acts of heroism he would go through for Mary Ann. He was getting quite fond of the lady and wasn't all that sure he wouldn't fight for her, if it became necessary. Of course, they were supposed to be just a summer dalliance, so he didn't really have any right to fight for her.

CHAPTER 15

Mary Ann was having so much fun, she worked on jewelry all morning and planning the grand opening in the afternoons. As well as getting everything they planned to sell, ready and priced and looking it's best. She sent advertisements to the town newspapers in the Chelan Valley and some further afield like Leavenworth and Wenatchee and even Seattle and Spokane. She sent ads to the online websites, too.

She had Tammy all trained and ready to go, and she'd asked all the artists if they could plan to be around the weekend of the grand opening, so people could ask questions and find out more about them. Nearly all of them said they would plan to attend a few hours each day.

Tuesday morning, she decided to grab some breakfast at Amber's restaurant, she'd been so busy at the gallery that she hadn't ordered any groceries and her fridge and cupboards were getting pretty bare, even her freezer was empty, except for some of Hank's beef. She had barely scraped together dinner last night and had immediately put in an order for groceries from Chelan, but she wouldn't get them until tomorrow. So today she was eating out, for breakfast at least.

When she got to Amber's restaurant she noticed there were a couple of police cars out front and a bunch of people on the sidewalk. She walked up to one of the groups of people milling about.

"What's up?"

Frank Miller, who owned the garage in town, shrugged. "I heard Amber was burglarized last night."

Mrs. Erickson, everyone's third grade teacher, put her hands on her hips. "Now don't you go spreading rumors Frank. We don't know anything for sure."

"Mrs. Erickson, I'm not spreading rumors, that's what Kimberly said when she told us it would be another half hour before they could open."

Mrs. Erickson frowned. "Yes, but you didn't hear it from Amber, so it's still a rumor. Second hand knowledge."

"But she's one of the waitresses…"

Mrs. Erickson interrupted him. "You should always check the facts before speaking. Do I need to remind you of the time when you were in my class and told everyone about…?"

Mary Ann was cringing inside for Frank, Mrs. Erickson had been the third-grade teacher of everyone in town over the age of eighteen. She'd taught for forty-seven years in their small town before she finally retired about ten years ago. And she had a mind like a steel trap, she never forgot one single embarrassing moment that happened in her classroom and she was happy to remind her former students of them at any time. She might forget she had cookies in the oven and set off her smoke alarm, but she never forgot anything that happened in her classroom.

Officer Ben Reynolds came out the door and interrupted Mrs. Erickson. "Hello folks, thanks for waiting patiently. Amber's restaurant had a burglary last night and we were just checking for any evidence. This is the third incident of burglary we've had in the town, so I want you all to start locking your doors and windows at night. And when you are away from home in the daytime, too. That goes for the businesses also. But now, Amber is open for breakfast."

After Mary Ann had eaten, she went directly to the studio, she wanted to tell Kristen what she had heard, and talk about what they might want to do to protect the gallery.

She was glad to find Kristen already at work when she arrived.

"Kristen, I just heard some very disturbing news and we need to decide what to do."

"What did you hear?" Kristen looked up from her work.

"Amber was robbed."

"Oh, my God, no! At gunpoint?" Kristen started to stand.

"What? No. Not robbed, I guess. She was burglarized. Someone broke into her restaurant last night after she closed and stole things. Food and dishes and utensils mostly."

Kristen relaxed back on her chair. "Oh, well that's not good, but better than being robbed. Still a loss, but not as scary as being held up by some whacko."

"Yes, sorry I don't often think about such things, so I don't think about the differences between the two. Anyway, officer Ben said it was the third incident in town and everyone needed to start taking better precautions at night. I got the impression the thief is coming in through open windows. Anyway, we should probably get some security in here."

"Yes, I think I would die if someone stole one of Lucille's art sculptures. Or anything really. It would be an awful feeling to lose someone's hard work."

"I think we need a security system and maybe a safe or something to lock the money in at night. I think I should start researching it first thing, rather than work on creating.

Maybe if I can find someone quickly I can get a little design time in afterwards." Mary Ann glanced wistfully at her spot on the workbench.

Kristen nodded. "That's probably a good idea. There is always tomorrow to work on producing new jewelry."

Mary Ann made calls all morning and found some good companies that would be able to supply what they needed. It would take a few days to get installed since they had to come in from outlying areas, but at least they had something on the way.

Mary Ann and Kristen were in the gallery at five when Tim Jefferson walked in. He was all dressed up, like he was going out on a date. How refreshing, that some kids still dressed up to look presentable for a job interview.

Mary Ann took the lead as she and Kristen had discussed earlier. "Thanks for coming in, Tim. Let's go have a seat in the office."

They all sat down together in the little office area they had set aside, it was just barely big enough for three chairs. They chatted for a bit to just get the feel for how comfortable he was talking to people. Then they tag-teamed him asking questions to see if he got flustered with more than one question at a time. Mary Ann asked him questions about the ranch while Kristen asked him questions about his art. He handled it all just fine and gave good answers.

"So, have you ever worked retail Tim?" Mary Ann asked him, this was pretty much the last question they had planned.

"No, can't say that I have. But I would really like to give it a try."

Kristen nodded. "You don't appear to be the silent stoic cowboy type, so as long as more than two people don't freak you out, I think we'd like you to have that try."

"No dad and Mike got the stoic silent thing going on, but me and Alyssa, not so much. Beth never met a stranger, she's the most talkative of all of us I think. Don't know who the twins will take after yet, maybe a split between them. Lance is already the spokesman, Vance is quieter."

Kristen stood. "Well, let's show you around then. I think you've got yourself a job here Tim."

Tim grinned. "Thanks, I'll work hard for you both."

They took Tim through the different areas of the gallery and told him as much as they could about the art and artists. Mary Ann planned to have him come back for a few more nights to get into the financial part. How different things would need to be wrapped for shipping and all the other things he would need to know. But they had the rest of the week, so she wasn't worried. They just had one area left to show him when Nolan walked in the door.

Kristen's eyes lit up when he ambled in. "Nolan, welcome, we're just showing Tim, our new evening employee, around."

"Tim, welcome to the best art gallery in town." Nolan shook Tim's hand.

Kristen laughed. "Easy for you to say since it's also the *only* art gallery in town."

"It would be the best, even if there were a dozen others." Nolan lifted one shoulder in a half shrug.

Mary Ann grinned at Nolan and said to Tim, "Come with me, let me show you the last area while Kristen talks to Nolan."

"Actually, the first order of business involves all of you. I wanted to come by to ask you about security measures for the gallery. We've had a string of small burglaries in town, at some of the local businesses. Most of them have just had a few small items stolen."

Mary Ann nodded. "We have heard something about that. Kristen and I talked about it this morning and have some things on the horizon. But it won't be in time for the grand opening."

They talked through the plans and what Nolan thought would be appropriate and promised to enhance their security further. When Kristen started to rant about how people were mean and being on her mountain was better, Mary Ann dragged Tim off and let Nolan listen to the rant.

"You'll hear all about her reclusive ideas later, lets wrap this up and head out."

Tim chuckled. "How many times have you heard it?"

She shook her head. "Many, many times. I could recite it in my sleep I think."

BRAVO TEAM WAS HEADING BACK toward Kristen's house for a short break and to replenish their packs. They were walking through a heavily burned out area, it was the most direct route back to the house they were borrowing, and it never hurt to go through a new area to check for any trouble they might find. The *Cat Box* was picking up Alpha team from further afield and Charlie team was on their way back out after having been to base for the last few days.

Trey climbed over a tree that had fallen blocking the way they were headed. In front of him was a large clearing that shouldn't really be there. They were in a heavily wooded area but there was nearly an acre of cleared land right in the middle of it. It looked like a garden, there were some corn stalks standing in places. Fire never truly burned everything in its path, it always left patches unharmed and there was clearly some corn growing. He looked around and saw what also looked like grape vines.

One of the other guys that had gone around the downed tree rather than climbing over it hollered out. "Hey, I found a cabin. I think."

The rest of the team moved toward his location, which was up on a bit of a rise. When Trey reached where Quinn and Finn were hunkered down, he couldn't see much of a cabin, but it did look like there had been some sort of structure. It wasn't a real large area, but maybe large enough for a one or two room cabin.

Finn said excitedly, "Look there are some shattered plates and some melted metal that might have been utensils. And a cast iron skillet that's just a little warped from the intense heat that probably came through here."

Kevin, their crew boss said, "Good detective work, Finn. I think we should probably record this location just in case. It's probably a hunting cabin or maybe fishing, since the stream isn't too far off."

Trey piped up. "I'm not so sure about that. I found about an acre of cleared ground that looks like it might have been a garden. There were definitely corn stalks and maybe some grape vines."

Kevin nodded. "Alrighty then, we better document this, everyone spread out and snap some pics on your phones, while I take down the coordinates. Try to estimate the size of the whole area that doesn't look normal."

Trey went back the way he had come and took Quinn with him. Finn and Kevin worked in the cabin area.

Quinn sighed. "That kid is going to be on cloud nine for finding that cabin."

Trey nodded. "Yeah, he is, fortunately, we're on our way back to base so he can drive Brandon crazy telling him the story. Over and over and over."

Quinn laughed. "Good point. And Alpha team will be right behind us, so he can drive them nuts too."

"Finn's twin is on Alpha team, so I imagine the twins getting together will help some, they'll go off in their twin world for a bit and give the rest of us a break."

"Oh, I hadn't thought about that, I hope the *Cat Box* hurries the hell up and gets Alpha team back first."

"No, I think Brandon being tormented for a couple of hours would be good for him."

Quinn shook his head. "With friends like you, who needs enemies?"

"Just looking out for my good buddy, since he didn't get to be here for all the excitement."

When the team regrouped to start back toward Kristen's house and their base of operations they decided that there was definitely someone living on the land. They'd found what looked like some cages, for maybe rabbits or chickens and what was quite possibly an orchard area, the fruit trees didn't seem to be indigenous to the mountain area, so they had to have been cultivated and looked to be at least ten years old. None of the team were experts on tree growth, but they tried to make educated observations.

This discovery would probably extend their debriefing time by a day or two, but they still should have a couple of days off, so they might be able to go into town.

CHAPTER 16

The day of the grand opening, Kristen and Mary Ann were as ready as they could get. Trey had surprised the crap out of her by sending them a huge spray of flowers from the Fighting Jaguars. She nearly burst into tears when they arrived and even Kristen got a little misty-eyed at their thoughtfulness.

As the time to open drew near, Mary Ann was so excited she could hardly breathe. Kristen, on the other hand, was a wreck. Tammy was there for the opening and Tim would be by later in the day. Mayor Carol and Gus got there early. Samantha had a snack station set up with drinks and cookies. She planned to do the serving to let everyone else help the people who came. They opened the doors at eleven, knowing the main ferry would arrive at eleven fifteen. The fast ferry should have landed earlier, but clearly, they had no one coming from that one.

Mary Ann was surprised when they didn't have anyone in the gallery at eleven thirty and even more surprised when the clock edged toward noon and only a couple of local people had come in. She wondered what had happened, she didn't believe for a minute that no one would be coming to the grand opening. But when no one did, she got concerned.

She saw Kristen leave and wondered if she should go after her when Nolan burst in the door.

"Get ready for customers everyone. There was an accident on the lake and both ferries stopped to help. It's cleaned up now and there is a bunch of people on their way. Some of them are stranded until they can get a ferry moving back up-lake, so there may be more people than expected."

"Mayor Carol, they wanted me to let you know, in case you wanted to go check it out. It's all settled, I think, but...."

Mayor Carol nodded. "Of course, I'll go over and see if anything is needed and come back here later. Gus, can you stay here and help out as needed?"

"You betcha, Mayor."

"Please tell Kristen, Nolan, she just left." Mary Ann pointed toward the studio.

He nodded and hurried out the back.

Mary Ann grinned. "Okay, like the man said, let's look sharp everyone."

The door opened, and people streamed into the gallery.

She barely had time to notice Kristen come back in a few minutes later. She already had a line of people asking questions and some were even ready to purchase. One woman she noticed had walked in given a cursory glance around, and made a beeline straight for the quilts Stephanie had brought in. She was already in line with her arms full. Behind her was a man with a claim ticket for one of Lucille's glass sculptures.

Mary Ann smiled to herself knowing their first day being open would be no less than a quarter of a million dollars in sales, just from the first two people in line. She started helping the customers as quickly as she could, answering questions, ringing up sales, and taking down mailing addresses for the larger items. She worked non-stop and every time she looked up the line had not shrunk any. It was going to be a long day.

Terry came up to the counter with a little boy who was about seven. The little boy looked up at Terry. "Thanks for helping me Mr. Terry, dad will be so surprised I got him something too."

Terry smiled at the kid. "My pleasure Shaun. Give this lady your things and she will ring them up to see how much they are and then you can pay her."

Shaun nodded and set his items on the counter. Mary Ann looked at his selections and started to add up the cost of them. She picked up the soap that Iris made, and Shaun said, "That's for my mom, it's her birthday tomorrow and she just loves fancy soaps. These smell really nice."

Mary Ann nodded. "They do, I have some myself and I love them."

"It's gonna be a surprise, daddy took mommy next door to see the costumes and dresses store, so I could buy these without her seeing. But dad doesn't know I'm getting him that carving of the bear. He just loves bears. I want to get me the little train that Mr. Terry made, but only if I have enough money. Mom and dad's presents come first."

Mary Ann smiled at him and was determined he would have enough money even if she had to help pay for them. "Well how much money do you have Shaun?"

The boy dug in his pockets and put all the wadded-up money on the counter with a handful of coins. Mary Ann counted it up and it almost paid for the parent's gifts, he was about thirty-five cents short. But it didn't touch Terry's toy train. She looked at Terry and he nodded.

"Well Shaun, that's almost exactly the amount you need for all these fine gifts."

She noticed him wilt, thinking he didn't have enough to

buy the train. Mary Ann pushed a quarter back towards him. "That is your change, now let me wrap these up for you so your parents can't see what you bought."

Shaun's face lit with pleasure and there was a suspicious wetness in Terry's eyes. What a softie the big man was. She carefully wrapped the gifts for the parents and put them in the bottom of the bag and then laid the toy train on top of some other tissue paper. So, it looked like there was only the train in the bag.

"There, that should do it. You will be able to surprise both of them."

Terry winked at her and then told Shaun he would walk him next door to Barbara's shop. When they were out the door, Mary Ann dug the sixty cents out of her purse that would pay for the adult gifts, she would square up with Terry later.

She still had a line of people wanting to check out.

TREY and the team were nearly back to base camp when they heard a commotion coming from a burned-out area, they cautiously moved toward that direction. There were squeals and hisses and thumps, as they got closer the sounds didn't change any, which was surprising, most animals quieted down when humans approached. They looked over some fallen trees into a small clearing where three raccoon kits were having quite the dustup. These looked a little too young to be alone without their mother, it would be another couple of months before they would be turned loose. The guys looked around to see if they could spot the mother while the kits fought.

Finn pointed. "There she is under that fallen tree, looks

like she's dead. Maybe the young ones are fighting over food."

Trey felt sorry for the youngsters, but wasn't quite sure what they could do, they didn't have the expertise to rescue them or help transplant them. They could mark the coordinates for the wildlife rescue people, but would the kits survive without the mother long enough for them to arrive?

Kevin frowned. "We're almost back to base, does anyone have any fruit they haven't eaten? We could leave that for the kits and then send in the wildlife people to decide what to do." Between the six of them they came up with enough fruit and granola bars to last the babies a few days. They unwrapped the nut and granola bars and gently tossed those and the fruit toward the raccoons. It caught one of the animals' attention and it went to investigate. It made some chattering noises and the other two stopped fighting and waddled over to the food.

Satisfied that the juveniles would be fine for a couple of days they headed back out toward the base. They had a lot to report with the burned-out homestead and the raccoon family.

CHAPTER 17

*M*ary Ann pulled up to the gallery, she loved this. She loved coming in each morning and setting up. She loved talking to people about the art. She loved selling it. She loved counting up the money, and there was a boatload of that coming in. She even loved cleaning up at the end of the day and taking the deposit to the bank. She did hope they would be able to get back to her doing more work, she needed to talk to Kristen about changing the hours just slightly, once the ferry was gone for the evening the place looked like a ghost town. One or two stragglers came in if they were staying in town, but the bulk of the people came in on the ferries. Tim would be able to handle the evening customers easily. She wondered if Kristen would mind if she spent the early evenings in the studio practicing. She'd have to... Shit what a mess!

The trash was dumped out on the ground, but not strewn around, just in piles. The trash cans were upside down in a pyramid. What in the hell? And the screen was off the window above that. Oh no! She ran around to the back entrance and that door was standing wide open. Kristen!

She ran in the back door yelling at the top of her lungs even as her hand punched in 911 on her cell. "Kristen! Kristen, are you alright! Kristen, where are you!"

Kristen opened the door at the top of the stairs that led to her living area, "Mary Ann, what's wrong."

"Oh, thank heavens, you're alright."

"Of course, I'm alright, what…"

Mary Ann raced up the stairs and pushed a startled Kristen back into her home as the dispatcher answered the phone and asked what the emergency was. "Michelle, I think Kristen's art gallery has been burglarized." When asked she rattled off the address, while she slammed the door into the gallery shut and locked it, with both the door lock and the deadbolt. "The back door was wide open and a window too." She pulled Kristen with her as she went to the back door to lock it and heard the dispatcher asking questions. "Yes, in the gallery, no I didn't touch anything. Yes, she seems to be fine. We're locked into the living quarters right now."

"Mary Ann, what in the fuck is going on?"

Mary Ann held up one finger as the dispatcher gave her final instructions. Then she hung up and sat down hard at the kitchen table, "I think we've been robbed, or burglarized, or…"

"What?" Kristen said moving towards the stairs into the gallery.

Mary Ann jumped up and grabbed Kristen's arm and dragged her back to the table. She pushed her into a seat and told Kristen to eat her toast and coffee while she explained.

"Right, okay, tell me what you saw."

"The trash is dumped out…"

"Oh, bears or raccoons…"

Mary Ann shook her head. "No. Now just listen. The trash is dumped out into piles. The trash barrels are in a pyramid up to that window we open for fresh air and the screen is off. And the back door was standing wide open."

"Oh, well yeah, not bears or raccoons then." Kristen finished speaking when someone started beating on the door. When Kristen let Nolan in he practically hugged the stuffing out of her. Several more townspeople came blasting in, mostly firefighters, who probably heard it over the police and fire scanner. Each of them grabbed Kristen in a hug until she snatched the radio mic Greg Jones had on his shoulder and told everyone she was fine and to calm down, using some colorful language that was not allowed on the airways.

Greg and Nolan went down to investigate while Mary Ann told everyone assembled what she had seen. Officer Ben came up a few minutes later and took statements from Mary Ann and Kristen. Kristen had awoken during the night and heard a few odd noises but hadn't thought anything of it and had gone back to sleep.

Chris who had heard what Kristen said to Ben frowned at her. "You heard odd noises in the building and didn't think to call the police to have them checked out even though you knew there had been burglaries in town?"

Kristen shrugged. "No, I was tired, and I didn't know the thump was in the building for sure. I just heard a thump."

Chris put his hands on his hips and scowled at her. "You heard a thump? Fine, but you still could have called the police to have them check on it."

"I live alone on the top of a mountain most of the time. I hear odd noises all the time and just ignore them. Or if I have to I get my shotgun out and scare them off. I don't have the luxury of calling the police."

Kyle pushed Chris back a little. Chris was normally a laid-back guy; Mary Ann had not seen him so agitated before. Kyle said, "We understand that Kristen, but you are living in town now and we've had some criminal behavior, and you really should have reported it."

Chris put his arm around Barbara when she huddled close to him.

Terry spoke up before Chris could. "We don't want you hurt, you probably just need to start thinking a little differently if you plan to live in town."

Kristen grimaced. "I haven't decided to live in town. It's much more peaceful on my mountain."

Barbara whispered, "But we like having you here." Then her eyes filled with tears and she hurried out of the room.

"Well hell, I didn't mean to upset her. You all know I love you, but I love my solitude too." Mary Ann understood Kristen was torn, but she agreed with Barbara, Kristen was a welcome addition to the town and their little circle of friends. Mary Ann would miss her nearly as much as her sister would, if Kristen returned to the mountain top.

Chris patted his sister in law on the shoulder. "It's okay, we just want you to be safe and we love having you around all the time." Kyle, Terry, and Mary Ann nodded, as Barbara came out of the bathroom and hugged her sister.

Then they all started talking a mile a minute speculating on what might have happened and why someone was breaking into the shops around town. Mary Ann wondered if this had something to do with Kristen's dog being sick and having to be taken to Chelan yesterday. If Kristen had stayed with her dog, the house might have been empty. She didn't know if she should mention it in the group or wait and ask Nolan or Kristen about it in private, maybe it was better to wait. She didn't want to add to the speculation running amok in the conversation.

Nolan came back a little while later to explain what they needed to do next. The most important job was to figure out what had been stolen, Chris, Terry and Kyle volunteered to help, since they had been in the gallery yesterday. Barbara said she was going over to her own shop since she would be no help downstairs, but she hugged Kristen again before she left. Mary Ann would have liked to do the same, but she and Kristen didn't have that kind of relationship, so she went downstairs with the guys to see if they could find out what all was missing.

～

THE REST of the trek back to Kristen's house was uneventful. Which in Trey's opinion was a good thing, they already had plenty to report. First their work on the fire had to be written up and relayed to those in charge of tracking everything. They had several weeks' worth of information to be recorded.

Second, they would need to report to not only the fire command, but also the town, the forest service, and maybe even the state, that they had found what looked like someone living off the grid. The report would have to be written on that and then the powers that be would send it out to the proper authorities.

Third they would need to report about the raccoon youngsters to the wildlife rescue people, so they could decide if they wanted to rescue the kits or let nature take its course. That would be a hell of a lot of meetings and debriefing before they had any time to themselves. Plus, they still needed to wash out their clothes and do any pack maintenance needed. His pack was fine, nothing had worn out while they were out.

When the three young raccoons waddled into Kristen's yard looking for more food, Trey was certain Kristen would not be pleased with the Fighting Jaguars. Mary Ann had mentioned that Kristen called them racoon armies. Apparently, the little beggars had followed the team's scent back to the base of operations. They were so darn cute and within hours became the unofficial mascots for the group, which meant putting them back out into nature was not going to be easy to accomplish. It was easy to become attached to them and let them get away with their shenanigans, when you didn't have to live with them. Trey hoped the wildlife people had some tricks up their sleeves, to reintegrate animals, that idiot firefighters allowed to become too domesticated.

CHAPTER 18

$\mathcal{T}$rey was so damn glad that they finally had been set free to go into town for a couple of days. He hadn't called Mary Ann to let her know he was coming, because the way they had been moving, like molasses in fricken' January, he wasn't quite sure they were going to have any time. He didn't want to disappoint her. But it looked like they would have two days and he felt lucky to get even that amount of leave. Trey decided by the time they got down the mountain it would be close to shift change at the gallery, and maybe he could just surprise her.

He kind of doubted she would be able to take much, if any, time off. The gallery had only been open a few days and the texts he'd gotten from her, which weren't many, had indicated they had been swamped. Which is probably why he hadn't gotten many texts, she was working like crazy. But he wasn't opposed to hanging out with her at the gallery and maybe chatting up some locals. He wondered if they had a gym he could work out in. What they did on the mountain was physical but didn't always work all the muscles like gym equipment was designed to do. So, he could keep himself occupied during the day and hang out with Mary Ann in the evenings.

He had the guys drop him off at the gallery, he was fairly certain Mary Ann would still be there. The rest of them were going straight to the bar for a beer, he wouldn't mind a beer, but he had a different kind of thirst he wanted to quench. One that only a pretty little wildcat could satisfy. He saw Mary Ann through the window. *Score, she is here.* He opened the door and he heard a small chime, Mary Ann turned her head and her eyes lit with pleasure. He didn't know where she was headed before, but she didn't hesitate to walk straight toward him.

"Trey, what are you doing here? Why didn't you call me? How long are you in town? Do you have time to be with me?"

Trey laughed at her running questions. "I'm in town to see you and I'm here until Wednesday morning, providing nothing happens on the mountain."

Her face lit up like the sun and she turned and thrust the cash box, in her hand, at Nolan who just barely caught it. "Tell Kristen I'm going to be deathly ill until Wednesday morning. Tammy and Tim will both be in so I'm sure they can handle the weekday people for two days."

Then she turned back to Trey and took his hand, he just grinned at Nolan and waved. Nolan shook his head and waved back, as she dragged Trey out of the building.

Once the door shut behind him Trey stopped and pulled Mary Ann back into his embrace. He gave her a warm kiss and hugged her close. She seemed to curl into him and he felt ten feet tall that she was so glad to see him walk into the building. He wanted to take her out for a little while to enjoy her company before they holed up in her house for the next forty-eight hours.

He pulled back and smiled at her. "So, I smelled something delicious in there, can I take you for dinner? Or have you already eaten? We could go have coffee or a drink."

She pouted a little. "You don't want to go to my house and play around?"

"Yes, I do, but I thought I could take you on a date first and we could chat, before you get deathly ill and have to stay home for the next two days."

She grinned at him. "We had a busy day, and I haven't eaten, Nolan just brought that food in before you came in, so I would be happy to go to dinner with you."

"Great, the café, pizza, teriyaki or bar food?"

"Let's go to the café, it has the most variety. Have you been there yet?"

"Nope, some sexy wench has kept me all to herself." He shook his head sadly.

She laughed. "All right, I will share you with the town for a few minutes while we eat. But after that, you may not see daylight for two days."

"You won't hear me complaining."

"Good, let's take my car, so we don't have to come back for it after."

She went over to the passenger's seat and started moving all kinds of stuff to the back. There was a box of tissues, and a sweater and two pairs of shoes. There were several water bottles, some were empty, and some were half full.

He laughed as she pulled more crap out of the little burnt orange Chevy Aveo. "It might be faster for me to walk and meet you there."

She took the snow brush off the floor and waved it at him. "Don't get sassy with me. I have a snow brush and know how to use it. This is the last thing, you can get in now."

He dropped his backpack into the backseat with all her crap, and got in. Then he pulled a butter knife out from under him. "You missed something. Do you butter toast in here often?"

"Oh, I had that in here to... never mind." She took it from his hand and stuck it in the door pocket.

Mary Ann started up her little car and then roared out of the parking lot. He wondered if she always drove like a crazy woman or if it was just because he was along. The little car had a lot of get up and go, which surprised him, it wasn't a sports car, just a little compact. She blasted around the corner and he was shocked the tires didn't squeal, he put his right hand casually down on the arm rest in the door and held on to the chicken bar in the handle. He didn't want her to notice, but at the same time he needed something to hold onto. The orange rocket raced down the street and up to the front of the restaurant where Mary Ann slammed on the breaks and casually put the car in park.

Trey released his white-knuckle grip on the door and eased out of the car. Just as they stepped into the restaurant one of the police officers who was leaving pointed at Mary Ann.

"Slow down. I'm not adverse to giving you another ticket, Mary Ann. You are single handedly paying for that new patrol car the department just purchased."

Mary Ann sighed and dropped her shoulders. "I will, I promise."

The officer shook his head. "You better." Then he looked at Trey. "You are a brave man, riding with that wild woman."

Trey shivered dramatically. "I didn't know."

The man guffawed and walked out the door.

Mary Ann crossed her arms. "I'm not that bad."

"Uh huh, which is why there are now my finger prints in the door handle."

The hostess asked, "Café or fine dining?"

There were two rooms one was a café, lunch counter and

salad bar. In the other room was white table cloths with candles on the table. He was torn between wining and dining Mary Ann, and the amazing looking salad bar. He liked salad, and that wasn't something he got a lot of, when he was on the hotshot locations.

Mary Ann took the decision away from him when she said, "Café. I've been working all day. I don't feel dressed up enough for fine dining."

Trey nodded, and they followed the hostess into the café side. "That salad bar looks great, how about we come back for the fine dining my last night in town and I can wine and dine you."

Mary Ann giggled. "You don't have to do that."

"I know, but I want to."

TREY WAS MAKING her feel so special, not like a hookup, he was treating her like a girlfriend and she was enjoying it. Maybe a little too much. But she decided she wasn't going to stop him, their time was short by necessity, so she wasn't going to waste a minute on negative feelings. She was simply going to enjoy the man and allow him to enjoy her, too. There was plenty of time after the fire season was over and he left, to deal with the negatives. She pushed those depressing thoughts far away into her subconscious and deliberately focused on the cute guy sitting across the table from her.

He looked up from his menu. "So, what's good?"

"Everything."

"Well that goes without saying. It's not a meal ready to eat or should I say choke down when it's the mystery meat. It's not jerky and it's not one of the hotshots cooking. By default, it's good, but what is your favorite?"

"I normally get whatever is the special for the day, just because it's not a standard from the menu. But from the standard things on the menu, the fried chicken is delicious, spaghetti is what you smelled at the gallery and it has home-made noodles and sauce, so it's very good. The steaks are from Hank's cattle ranch, they are terrific, as is the meatloaf."

Trey's eyebrows rose. "Meatloaf, really?"

"Yep, it starts with the best beef you've ever tasted and just gets better from there."

"Well in that case I have to try it. I've never had a meatloaf I didn't like, well except for the mystery meat in the MREs."

Mary Ann nodded. "It's a great choice, but Nolan brought in spaghetti and my brain settled on that, so I'm going to have to get some, the meatballs are to die for and the cook makes a sauce that he simmers all day."

"Sounds tasty, but you've sold me on the meatloaf."

"I could be persuaded to give you a bite or two."

"Are you willing to take a chance on a payment after sharing, rather than persuasion before it?" he said with a sly smile.

She felt heat rise in her cheeks as she realized what he was implying. The waitress came up to take their drink orders.

Mary Ann spat out, "Ice water, lots of ice water."

Trey laughed at her reaction. "I'll have iced tea, thanks."

When the waitress left, Mary Ann shook her finger at him. "Now you stop that right now, this is a family restaurant."

"Fine, but I didn't say anything at all that would be offensive, it was all in your imagination. Your mind took you to those naughty places, not my words."

She frowned as she thought back over his words, then she pointed at him again. "But you meant what I thought. I know you did. So, stop it."

Trey laughed again, stood and held out his hand to her. "Let's get some salad. That should be innocent enough."

She shook her head and said sadly, "If only that were true."

They loaded up at the salad bar, she was an exotic lettuce lover, and he liked plain old iceberg or romaine. She teased him about eating his boring salad, and he teased her right back about being an uppity salad eater and too good for the likes of him.

WHEN THE WAITRESS brought out their main course Trey wondered if maybe he should have skipped the salad. His portion of meatloaf looked large enough to feed a small family.

Mary Ann laughed at his expression of distress and whispered, "Don't worry, Hotshot. We'll take the extra home, for sandwiches."

He liked the way she called her house their home. He might be able to get used to that. If he didn't need to go back to his own state. That idea wasn't sounding nearly as appealing as the end of fire season normally did. "Thank God for that, there is no way I could eat it all."

Mary Ann giggled. "Yeah, Amber's cook loves to pile it on, especially when there is a new guy in the restaurant. You being a hotshot probably gave him even more incentive."

Trey looked around to see if someone was watching. "How does he know there is a new guy and that he's a hotshot?"

"It's a small-town thing." She said as she patted his hand like he was three.

While they ate, they debated which of her Sci-Fi collection they should delve into for the next two days. The meatloaf was delicious as were the bites of spaghetti and meatballs she shared with him. When he couldn't eat another morsel, he laid his fork down and patted his very full stomach.

"That was delicious, but I'm stuffed, and at least half of the meatloaf I didn't even touch."

She looked at him with a gleam in her eye that he didn't understand. "The leftovers will make yummy sandwiches tomorrow. But I hope you aren't too full."

He groaned when the waitress set down in front of him, the largest piece of chocolate French silk pie he'd ever seen.

Mary Ann grinned at him. "It's the house specialty, something passed down through Amber's family for generations. You'll have to have a few bites now, but we can take the rest home."

He picked up his fork and thought again how he liked that word coming out of her mouth. "Are you going to help me with this?"

She just smiled at him while he took a tiny bit of pie and put it in his mouth. Trey thought he had died and gone to heaven it was so delicious. "That is amazing, maybe I won't share after all."

She grinned. "Yeah, I thought you might feel that way. Too bad." Mary Ann laughed as she speared a large bite of the pie and stuffed it in her mouth.

They both had several more mouthfuls but didn't come close to finishing it. The waitress brought out three take home boxes and a bag to carry it all. After they had all the food boxed up and the bill settled, Trey remembered he had to get in the speed demon's car.

"Um, I think maybe I should walk back to your place, to um, walk off some of the food. I could meet you there." He said hopefully.

She batted her green eyes at him. "Now you aren't

nervous about my driving, are you? A big bad wildfire fighter can't possibly be scared of little ol' me, can you?"

He debated between losing his man card and getting in the orange rocket.

Before he could decide, Mary Ann patted him on the chest. "Don't worry, Hotshot. One of Chedwick's finest is parked right outside waiting for me to come out. I can't afford another ticket, so I will drive slowly. Like an old man in a hat."

"I might have to commend that guy for saving many lives, starting with mine."

CHAPTER 19

*M*ary Ann drove sedately to her house, well sedately for her anyway. When she turned off her car Trey sighed like he'd had to endure torture. She rolled her eyes. "Come on scaredy cat, let's go in."

"Not scared. I just have a healthy desire to live. You and your orange rocket are in direct opposition to that desire."

She guffawed. "Orange rocket. I love it! I'm going to start calling it that, and then I can blame my driving on you, for putting ideas in my head."

"Great, that's all I need, you causing fear in my name."

She looked over at him and licked her lips. "Don't worry about that I'll make it up to you in advance."

Grinning at her, he said, "In that case why are we sitting in this death trap?"

She huffed. "It's not a death trap, it's my little orange rocket. Grab the food, we've got a lot of lovin' waiting on us inside."

The man could really move when he was motivated. He had the food in one hand, a back pack in the other, and was out the door and standing on the porch before she could get the keys out of the ignition.

"Come on woman, let's get this lovin' started. I've only got two days..." he waggled his eyebrows "... and three nights."

Laughing at his impatience, she unlocked the door.

"I see you're locking it now," he said with a nod toward the key.

"Yes. Since the burglaries around town started I've been locking it. I hope they find out what's going on. It's kind of sad to have to lock everything up all the time."

He shrugged and followed her in the door. "I hope you continue to lock it even after they find out who's stealing things. It's safer for you, especially since you're seeing an influx of tourists."

She sighed. "I suppose you're right, but I don't have to like it."

He kissed her on the nose. "But you locking up, will give *me* peace of mind. I'll put this food in the fridge."

"You do that while I get comfortable. Come find me when you're done being domestic."

"It won't take me a minute," he said and took off in a rush.

She giggled and hurried to her bedroom. Time for the fun to begin.

TREY CAREFULLY PUT the food in the fridge. He checked to make sure the backdoor was locked and then wondered if she'd actually secured the front door, so he went back to verify that it was indeed bolted. When he got to the bedroom Mary Ann was nowhere in sight, so he decided to give her a minute, he figured she was in the bathroom.

He dropped his backpack of extra clothes in a corner and

stripped out of everything except his jeans. When he turned around he about swallowed his tongue, Mary Ann was wearing an extremely hot outfit that was a parody of the uniforms from one of their favorite science fiction shows. It was skin tight and so short it just barely covered the essentials. It was also low cut in the front giving him a tantalizing peek into paradise. He stood there frozen while she gave him a naughty look and ran her hands over her breasts and down her sides.

She sauntered over to him on stiletto heels. "So, I take it you like my little outfit."

He couldn't say a word but managed to nod woodenly.

She ran one finger down the middle of his chest to his waistband and hooked that finger into his jeans and tugged him forward. "I didn't buy it and put it on, for you to stand there like a statue, Hotshot. Now let's have some fun."

He swallowed, but his throat was still dry as a bone. She fastened ruby red lips on his, and kissed him until he had no brain cells left firing. All his blood had flowed south.

He did manage to get his hands on her ass, and pull her forward, so she could feel just exactly what that hot outfit had done to his body. She purred and rubbed against him and he was certain his eyes rolled back in his head from her actions.

The woman was trying to kill him with lust and doing a damn fine job of it. She unbuckled his belt and unfastened his fly, pushed his jeans and shorts down and fastened those ruby red lips on another part of his anatomy, while he held on for dear life.

When he could take no more of her exquisite torture he pulled her up and lifted the tiny skirt up, finding her bare underneath it. He managed to grab a condom and roll it on before he impaled her up against the wall.

She wrapped her legs around his waist and clung to him

while he pounded into her. She met him with each stroke, and they came together in an explosion that he was certain would knock the house off its foundation. He managed to stumble the few steps to the bed, and they fell onto it in a heap with him still inside her.

A little while later she moaned. "Well, that was worth every penny I paid for it."

He chuckled. "And I will never be able to watch that show again with any sort of composure."

She sighed. "Mission accomplished. We can make it our goal to watch the whole series over the next two days."

He groaned. "Are you trying to kill me?"

"Man up, Trey, let's see some of that famous hotshot endurance."

He growled and rolled her under him. "I'll show you endurance." Then he fastened his lips on hers and kissed the breath out of her.

FOR THE NEXT two days they tried to one up each other. To see who had the most endurance and creativity while watching the DVDs, and adding in a lot more steam than anyone ever attributed to the original show.

On their last night together, Trey coaxed her into getting dressed up, so he could take her out for dinner. As she'd promised him Sunday night, they had not left her home for forty-eight hours. But he made a big deal about wanting to take her out, so she'd dragged on a pretty dress and they went to Amber's fine dining area for dinner.

Amber met them at the door with a smirk. "So, you are finally emerging from being *deathly ill* for two days. Funny you don't look the least bit sick. In fact, you look quite healthy."

Mary Ann laughed at her friend. "Trey gave me lots of TLC and I survived the *illness* quite well. But now he's determined to wine and dine me, so we'll take a table in fine dining. In a corner away from everyone else if you have one." She winked at Amber and gave her a naughty look.

Amber barked out a laugh. "So, he can continue the TLC? No hanky panky in my restaurant, Mary Ann Thompson. This is a family place. Maybe I should put you in the middle of the room to discourage anything."

"That wouldn't be a wise course of action, Amber. A dark corner would suit us better." Mary Ann moved closer to Trey.

Trey stepped back and took her by the arms holding her away from him. "Anywhere is fine, Amber. I'll keep her under control. As much as I can, anyway."

Amber laughed. "Good luck with that, Mary Ann is a force of nature."

He grinned. "Don't I know. I had to practically drag her out of the house as it is."

"It's not my fault. I don't want to share him," she whined.

Amber rolled her eyes. "Don't wear him out too much, Mary Ann. He has to go back to fighting fires tomorrow. Follow me."

Amber hooked them up with a semi-secluded table. Not exactly a dark corner but not out with everyone else either. It had some large plants on one side that made it seem cozy. They spent a very enjoyable evening having a few glasses of wine, some really great food and even better conversation. He talked about his family and job and how he got in with the hotshots to begin with. She told him about her upbringing and living in this tiny town. The good and the bad.

After dinner and amazing dessert, they went back to her house and spent a long time making love. When she drifted off to sleep it was with a smile on her face and a song in her heart. The man was a keeper, and she was happy to have been allowed this short time to enjoy him.

CHAPTER 20

The workshop was empty when Mary Ann floated into it Wednesday morning. Which surprised the heck out of her, she'd rarely arrived at the studio and not found Kristen hard at work. She looked out the door toward the back entrance to Kristen's apartment and saw the reason Kristen was nowhere to be seen. Nolan's car was parked back there.

Mary Ann smirked. "Well, well, well, something has finally distracted our little work-a-holic." Of course, she had no room to talk, since she'd been MIA for two glorious sex-filled days. She happily went over to her workstation and found a note from Kristen.

Mary Ann, Nolan and I are out taking Farley around town to see if he acts different toward anyone. Maybe the person who poisoned him with what the vet thinks was mushrooms might have left his scent.

So, we are going to see what we can see. Don't know what time I'll be back, so you're on point in the gallery.

Call if needed. TTYL, Kristen

Poisoned with mushrooms, well that confirmed her suspicion on Farley getting sick right before the break in. Now Kristen was out playing detective. The woman never slowed down. Shaking her head, she got out the jewelry she had been working on before the grand opening had shut down everything else. It would be fun to get back to making things again.

As she got everything out she thought about her few days with Trey. They seemed to be very compatible in so many ways. She kind of wished he didn't live so far away. But no, she wasn't really interested in long term, the fact that they had a time limit made it so much easier to go for what she wanted, and it also gave them both a bit of desperation to wring every bit of enjoyment out of every minute. They didn't have time for games or reticence. It actually made everything seem more vibrant and alive. She was having what could possibly be the best time of her life.

Mary Ann really liked what they were doing, and if her heart was a tiny bit wistful for more, well she would just ignore that. The torch in her hand lit on the first strike. She turned the flame to the size she wanted it and aimed it toward the piece of silver she had liberally doused with the boric acid and denatured alcohol solution, Kristen had taught her to use with silver. Silver liked to turn pretty colors when heated, as the impurities in the metal came out, it was kind of pretty as it happened, but it didn't look so great on a finished piece.

They were going to have a busy week. The security people were coming tomorrow, finally. A little too late, since they'd already had stuff stolen. But as Trey had pointed out, they did have a lot of new people in town with the amusement park being so well received, therefore it was a good idea to have more security. A little cash box and a few glass jewelry cases wasn't secure at all. A couple of safes and a security system would be much better. She wondered how much the installation would disrupt the gallery being open. Although she didn't really expect a lot of people, with it being mid-week.

TREY and all three Fighting Jaguar teams were at Kristen's house for a change in their assignment. They hadn't been on the line long after their last few days off in town. The burn out that they hoped would keep Chedwick and the outlying homes safe from the fire was finished. So, they had been brought in for reassignment. Not to a different fire, which was always a possibility, but a change in location at this job.

Often when they were being moved, they had a few days off, but not this time. So, no trip into town, which was a darn shame, because Trey would have been happy to have a bit more time with Mary Ann. But he was here to do a job, not hang out with the pretty locals. The current challenge was further up-lake near Lucerne, and all three hotshot companies were going to be tackling it. The Entiat and Baker River teams from the Lucerne side, and the Fighting Jaguars from this side. The Smoke Jumper team was fighting it from the west where it was too rugged to get into without air support. The fire was threatening the towns of Lucerne and Holden now, so the other two companies would be defending the towns while the Fighting Jaguars would come in from behind and try to create more fire breaks. There were a couple of campgrounds that needed a fire break between them and the monster wreaking havoc.

They were going to be at Kristen's less than 24 hours,

long enough to shave, shower, switch out their filthy clothes for some clean ones and restock their food. He planned to call or text his family, check on his business emails and maybe call Mary Ann, just to say hi.

There would be a briefing on what to expect in an hour. Then they would spend the night at the house and head out first thing in the morning. Trey was working in the living room of Kristen's house on his pack and cleaning up his equipment, when there was a knock on the door. Odd, who would be knocking on the door? He went to answer it and found Nolan on the porch.

"Hi Nolan, whatcha doing all the way up here?"

"I was wondering if Kristen had come up."

"Nope, haven't seen her, although I do think it's probably safe for her to move back up now. We've got the area as safe as we can make it." Trey was a little confused by Nolan's question, he was certain Mary Ann had told him Kristen and Nolan were an item. "I thought you and Kristen were pretty tight."

Nolan's ears turned pink. "Yeah, we were, but I kind of broke it off, and now I need to talk to her in an official capacity."

Trey was surprised to hear that Nolan had broken it off with Kristen. Mary Ann had talked like they were living in each other's pocket. "Oh, didn't Mary Ann know where she was?"

"When I stopped by the gallery Mary Ann wasn't there, only Tim, and he didn't seem to know anything."

Trey looked at his watch. "Oh, yeah, it is late enough for Mary Ann to be off. Doesn't Kristen have a sister? Maybe you could ask her."

"I will, thanks Trey. Where are you guys going now that you've got our little corner of the world secure?"

"Further up-lake, the monster is bearing down on

Lucerne and Holden Village and those camp grounds between here and Domke Lake. We've got three hotshot crews working on it and a fire jumper crew. If we can just get it contained and not spreading, we'll be happy. We'd rather not have to call in other hot shot crews, we're spread a little thin this year with all the forest fires. It's been a tough season. Not sure the darn thing will be completely out until the first snow fall."

Nolan whistled. "That's not any time soon. Well good luck to you."

"Thanks Nolan. Good luck finding Kristen."

As Trey watched Nolan head back to his patrol car he wondered about their breakup. Relationships were hard sometimes, but at least they lived in the same town, not like him and Mary Ann. He and Mary Ann didn't stand a chance, of course the lady had never acted like she wanted any kind of relationship. In fact, she often pointed out that it was nothing more than a fling, which if he was honest with himself, he would admit, that stung a little. He was a good guy, yeah, he lived in another state, but it wasn't like he was totally tied down there, his business could be done from anywhere. And his family was spread out to where they only got together a few times a year for holidays and sometimes vacations. They kept in touch mostly over electronic devices.

MARY ANN WAS JUST SITTING down in front of the television, with her dinner, when her phone rang. She looked at the display and was surprised to see it was Trey calling, he almost never called her, and he'd only been back out in the field a few days. She hoped there was nothing wrong.

She hit answer. "Hi Trey. Why are you calling me? You never call me. Is something wrong?"

"Hello pretty lady. Nothing to worry about, we got finished with the fire break today, so they pulled us in to relocate us."

At that news Mary Ann's heart sank, she knew he could be relocated at any time, but she was still enjoying his company and would be sad to have him moved to another fire. "Well I'm glad to hear our town is safe," she said trying to sound cheerful.

"Yeah, Kristen could probably move back up here if she wanted to. They're sending us further up-lake to some camp grounds and stuff near Domke lake. The fire is threatening that area now and some little towns named Holden and Lucerne. We're gonna fight it from the south and there are some other crews coming down from the north."

Yay, he isn't leaving the area! She was a little surprised at the force of her relief and tried to sound calm. "I hope you can get it under control, there aren't a lot of people up there, but the retreat is used a lot."

"I'm not sure if I'll have any cell reception while we're up there, but I'll text when I can. So, how's it going at the gallery?"

"Good. They arrested the kid that was breaking into the businesses in town. He was the one living in that area you guys found. From the scuttle butt I heard, his father abducted him when he was little and brought him here to hide him from his very rich mother. The dad died a few years ago, but the kid didn't know anything except living on the land. When the fire forced him out, he found the town and was stealing things to survive. It's a very dramatic story. I'm waiting to see the write-up in the newspaper, maybe tomorrow. They have to clear it with the mother first since he's a minor. I understand she's on her way to town."

"Wow, you've had an exciting couple of days. So that's probably why Nolan came by looking for Kristen."

"Nolan came up there?"

"Yep."

"Won't do him any good. She's on her way to some gem shows to buy some new stock. It's my understanding she goes every year, although it seemed like a rather sudden decision. I didn't think she was planning to go this year, and then she just left this morning."

"Probably was after she and Nolan broke up."

"Wait. What? She and Nolan broke up? When was that?"

"I don't know, he said he was looking for her and when I questioned him he said that he had broken up with her. Oh, hold on a sec, I have another call."

She got dead air for about a minute before he came back.

"Mary Ann, it's my sister I need to talk to her."

"Of course, you do. Thanks for calling."

"I've got another briefing in fifteen minutes, so I won't be able to call you back. I'll be in touch as soon as I can."

"Be safe." It was on the tip of her tongue to end the conversation differently, but she fought the urge.

She was grinning as she got ready for bed. It had been a fun, but short, conversation. She was happy he had called, but a little disappointed the call had been cut short. But she figured his family worried about him, so she couldn't begrudge his sister for calling.

He had a tight knit family with both parents still alive and three sisters. She guessed fire season must be hard for them with him being gone all summer. They probably missed seeing him every day. He was a good man, and if things were different, she might wish their relationship could be something more than a summer fling. But it wasn't different, so she would enjoy what she had for the summer and be glad for the experience.

CHAPTER 21

*M*ary Ann was so glad to have life back to normal, almost three weeks had been a long time to hold down the fort while Kristen was gone. She was finally back from her gem buying trip and she'd made up with Nolan. All those rumors about Kristen hooking up with some gem cutter named Sam were just bunk. Sam turned out to be short for Samantha, everyone had chuckled at their silliness for believing rumors.

Kristen all but floated into the studio almost an hour after Mary Ann had arrived. Mary Ann made a big show of looking at her arm and pretending to have a watch there.

"Well it's about time you showed up for work, young lady." Mary Ann waggled her finger at Kristen.

Kristen grinned at her. "You're just jealous."

Was she jealous? Maybe she was, a little. She huffed. "Well yes, maybe I am, but still, you used to always be in here before me. Not so much lately."

"No, but sadly that will all change next week when Nolan goes back on mornings, and I don't have anyone subverting my attempts at getting ready. That man can be very persuasive."

Mary Ann shook her head. "Changing the subject now. Are you guys going to the fire department picnic on Sunday?"

Kristen's eyes sparkled with mischief and she laughed. "Oh yes, it will be Nolan's first time. I can hardly wait." She cackled with glee and rubbed her hands together.

"Oh my, poor Nolan, are you bringing him an extra pair of clothes?"

"I haven't decided. It might be good for him to sit around in freezing cold jeans for a while. It might cool down some of the ardor."

Mary Ann raised her eyebrows. "Then again he might want you to help him warm up afterward."

"Hmm, I hadn't thought about that. Now I have to decide if that's a good thing or a bad thing."

"Just bring the man some clothes." Mary Ann put her hands on her hips.

"I know they've invited the Fighting Jaguars. Now whether they'll be able to join in the fun is anyone's guess. Have you heard from Trey?"

Mary Ann shook her head. "Not too much, the cell service up there isn't so great. They aren't close enough to Lucerne to tap into their tower and too far away from here. Kind of in a dead man's zone. I get an occasional flurry of texts that he has clearly sent over several days. But I haven't heard how it's going there, I mean I see the podcast updates, but it doesn't tell me much about how the crews are doing or when they'll get a break."

"No, the updates are for residences and smoke levels and things like that, not concerned girlfriends."

"Oh, I'm not a girlfriend. I mean we're just having a fling.

A summer fling, kind of thing. Nothing serious. Or permanent. Or..."

Kristen held up her hand. "Got it, let me rephrase. The podcasts aren't for friends with benefits, or maybe I should say fuck buddies. Is that better?"

"Ah, sure." Mary Ann was a little taken aback by Kristen's statement. She hadn't thought about it like that. Is that all they were to each other? She didn't really like those descriptions, but maybe Kristen was right. It sure looked different with that terminology, she much preferred a summer fling.

SUNDAY MORNING, Trey was surprised to be heading back down-lake to Chedwick. Yes, they had been working straight through for 3 weeks and yes, a couple of days down time was really needed, but the fire was still harassing the edges of Holden village. The teams had gotten a handle on keeping it from Lucerne, the Domke lake area and the camp grounds along the edge of Lake Chelan. But Holden was so remote that there was a lot of potential for ignition, it wasn't really a town at all but a Christian retreat, where the original town of Holden had been. When they closed the copper mine the miners and their families had left the area, and the Lutheran church had set up the retreat. With the abandoned copper mine, there was a lot of cut timber just waiting for flame. The other two hot shot divisions were still holding the fort up in that area.

He wasn't sure where the Fighting Jaguars were headed after a couple of days in Chedwick. But for the next two days he wasn't going to worry about it. First stop was the fire station where they would all get cleaned up and then they were invited to the town's volunteer firefighters picnic. Which was more of a whole town picnic, since everyone was invited. Mary Ann had mentioned it and said the town basically shut down for the day. It was the culminating event of the summer and the kids would go back to school the following week.

From the stories Mary Ann had told him about the volunteers, they were a rowdy bunch and loved to play pranks on each other. He'd met a lot of them the night the bakery had caught on fire. That seemed like a life time ago, but it had only been a couple of months. How things had changed from that night. When he had been fighting his attraction to Mary Ann, for her own good of course. He snorted at his foolishness. He could hardly wait to see her in a few hours at the picnic. He had decided to surprise her by just showing up.

Trey was impatiently waiting for his turn in front of the mirror, he'd managed to snag a shower pretty quickly, but with twenty guys all trying to shave and shower, it was taking forever to cycle through them. The fire department wasn't set up for that many people to try to use all at the same time. He was starting to wish he hadn't decided to surprise Mary Ann and had gone over to her house to get cleaned up. But he wanted to be clean and shaved and maybe he could even stop and get her some flowers, if the store was open.

He'd thought a lot about the two of them while he was up-lake and he had decided he needed to romance her some. He enjoyed their time together, but it seemed a little shallow for the way he was starting to feel about her.

Finally, he was on his way to the park, showered, shaved and in clean clothes. The flower shop had been closed, but the tourist trap also known as the general store was open. So, he'd stopped in to see if he could buy her something pretty. He'd found some pretty silver earrings with a pearl that dangled from the crescent shaped metal.

The store had pretty boxes, so he'd had the earrings put in the pretty box.

When he got to the park he wandered through the huge number of people who seemed to be everywhere. There was a bunch of tables set up as a buffet line, that had enough food to feed the state of Washington. There was a half-dozen stock tanks filled with ice and drinks. Everything from water and soda to beer. He'd noticed the beer was being closely watched by Greg, to keep the drinking legal. He grabbed a bottle of water and said hi to the people he recognized from town, but he still hadn't seen Mary Ann yet.

There was a fierce competition on the baseball field and some of the older guys were even playing horse shoes. He didn't know anyone still played that game. He didn't see many people on their phones which surprised the heck out of him, even the teenagers were engaged in the party. Frisbees were flying through the air and the little kids were playing on the swings and a climbing structure that kind of looked like a dragon. He decided that must be the infamous Tsilly the Lake Monster. He kept walking and found an area set up where people were making homemade ice cream, with hand crank machines. That stopped him in his tracks, was there some sort of time warp in this town like Brigadoon?

When he turned around he saw Kristen and Nolan, so he went over to ask them if they knew where Mary Ann was.

Nolan grinned and shook his hand. "Good to see you, Trey."

"Good to be seen. Hi Kristen, do you guys know where Mary Ann is? I can't find her in this crowd."

Nolan pointed to Trey's right. "Yeah, we just saw her over by the dessert table, she brought her world-famous brownies."

Kristen elbowed Nolan and Trey wondered what that was about but set off in the direction Nolan had indicated. He heard Nolan ask why she had done that and heard Kristen whisper something that started with Mary Ann. He had no idea what was going on and didn't care, he was a man on a mission. Right up until he finally saw Mary Ann, and then he saw nothing but red, or maybe green.

She was right in front of him and some guy was all over her. And she didn't seem to be fighting him off. She wasn't exactly reciprocating, and she was speaking to him in a quiet voice. But what was this guy doing with his girl. Maybe she wasn't really his girl on a permanent basis, but he thought she was at least his girl for the summer. Well to hell with that. He started to turn on his heel to get the hell out of there before he did something crazy.

But then he heard Mary Ann say. "Enough Steve. Trey, there you are, I'm so glad you made it." Then she turned back to the Steve guy and said to him, "That's my date, Steve. Now if you'll excuse me."

She pushed past Steve who whined at her leaving, rushed over to Trey and took his arm. He realized she was shaking and wondered if it was shaking mad or shaking in fear, regardless he pulled her in close, and led her off to a quiet spot to talk and decompress.

When they were far enough away from the crowd, he asked, "Who was that guy."

"Someone I dated for five minutes in high school. Most of the time he's fine, but occasionally he has too many beers and gets pushy with one of us women. One of the other girls would have noticed and come help to me, if you hadn't shown up. He's a coward so another woman or a man sends him running. His older brother is much more aggressive, fortunately he lives in Seattle, so we don't see him much."

That pissed him off, he didn't like men that treated women poorly, he had too many sisters to put up with that nonsense. "I got the idea that Kristen had seen you with him. Why didn't she and Nolan do something?"

"Good question. I think it's probably because Steve only harasses women younger than he is. Kristen is a couple of years older. She has lived up on the mountain for years and probably is unaware of his behavior."

"Someone should clue Nolan in at least, he's a police officer, he should know to keep an eye out." He glanced around to see if he could spot the officer.

"That's probably not a bad idea. But can we just go back to the beginning today and start over?"

He raised an eyebrow. "What did you have in mind."

"This." She jumped into his arms, wrapped her arms around his neck and her legs around his waist. He had quick reflexes, so he braced himself and tightened his hold to keep her from falling.

She said, "Trey, you're here! Why didn't you tell me you were coming? You could have come to my house to clean-up and I could have helped you. Maybe scrub your back or something." She squirmed against him.

He swatted her lightly on the butt. "Now stop that, we're in a public place."

"My point exactly. If you had come to my house, we wouldn't have been in public." She squirmed again. And started kissing him all over his face.

He gritted his teeth and growled, "Woman."

She laughed delightedly. "It's your fault."

He sighed and realized maybe his plan had not been such a great one after all. "I wanted to surprise you. And if you'll stop climbing me like a tree, I have a present for you."

She squirmed again and grinned at him. "I can feel it. But like you said, we're in a public place, so now you're going to have to wait hours and hours and hours, to give it to me."

He swatted her on the butt again. "Not that present, a real one. Now get down so I can give it to you."

She squirmed one more time and slid down his body to stand on her own two feet. He was glad his back was to the crowd, so no one could see the state all her squirming had put him in. He got the backpack off his shoulder that had a change of clothes and a few necessities to spend the night with her, if she invited him to, which seemed like a done deal from all her talk and squirming.

He unzipped the front pocket and pulled out the pretty box. Her eyes lit up with delight and he decided maybe his plan had been a good one after all. He handed her the box, and she clutched it tight. "Open it."

She lifted the lid and moved the paper to the side and then looked at him with the oddest expression he'd ever seen, like she didn't know whether to laugh or cry. She flipped one of the earrings to the back and laughter won. It started with a giggle, that morphed into a chuckle, she snorted and then hooted with laughter. She laughed and laughed until she couldn't stand any longer and collapsed to the ground, practically rolling with laughter. He had no idea what was so funny, but she just kept laughing. She would start to get herself under control and look up at him to explain and then it all started over again. He didn't know what to do. Her face got red from so much laughing, he was starting to be afraid she would pass out from lack of oxygen. Tears were streaming down her face. People started closing in on them to see what was so funny, that Mary Ann was on the ground laughing like a loon. He just shrugged at the looks he got.

Finally, Kristen showed up and asked, "What the hell is so damn funny that it's disrupting the whole picnic?"

Trey said, "I have no idea. I gave her that gift and she burst out laughing."

Mary Ann held the box up to Kristen, still laughing, although she was finally breathing again, and her face wasn't so red. Kristen took the box and moved the paper to the side and chuckled. Then she patted him on the chest. "Well, you have good taste anyway."

"What is it?"

"Mary Ann made these earrings." Kristen flipped it over like Mary Ann had done and let out a bark of laughter. Mary Ann pointed at the box, nodded and started laughing again. "It's the first pair she ever made. She made them the day after your first weekend with her. See the little number one on the back? I always number my creations and had her do that too. We had just finished girl-talking about that weekend."

Now it was Trey's turn to have a red face, as he thought about that weekend of nearly non-stop sexcapades.

Kristen laughed. "Don't worry, Hotshot. It wasn't that explicit." Then Kristen turned to the crowd. "Back to the picnic folks, just a bit of irony for our Mary Ann." She handed Trey the box of earrings and herded the crowd away from them.

Trey sat down on the grass next to Mary Ann. He didn't know what to say or even what to think. It was kind of ironic, his first and only gift to her was something she made, but the fact that she made them right after their first weekend and after she had talked to Kristen about it was pretty incredible. There had been a lot of earrings on that stand he could have chosen. What were the odds he would pick that exact pair?

Mary Ann reached for him, pulled him down to her and put her warm mouth on his in a searing kiss. When they finally broke apart she said, "Thank you, that was very sweet of you." Her eyes were filled with mirth. "And quite the keepsake. Plus, I got my abs training for the next week."

"Do you want me to take them back and get you something different?"

"Oh no, I love it. I will treasure them always." She took them from his hand and put them on, in place of the ones she'd worn. She handed him the box to put back in his backpack.

CHAPTER 22

*M*ary Ann was touched by the gift Trey had given her. It was sweet of him to think about giving her a gift. The fact that the earrings were so significant was highly amusing, but even during all the laughter there had been some regret, that this pair of earrings would be all she would keep of him. That and some memories. It had tinged the laughter with a little bit of hysteria, as she had thought about all it meant. She was glad no one had caught on to that part of the laughter and had taken it for irony only, but she knew there had been more to it.

She was still determined not to let anything distract her from enjoying every minute she had with Trey, so she pushed the sadness to the side and stood up. "So, let's go eat some of that yummy food I smell cooking on those grills the town assembled. You've been eating MREs and rations for about three weeks now, I'll bet your stomach would be happy for some real food."

Trey stood, shouldered his back pack, took her hand and they walked back to the picnic. They loaded their plates with food, there was every kind of meat known to man on the grills, with the beef overwhelming all the others, with hamburgers, beef ribs and several different cuts of steak. The tables were filled with all kinds of salads, chips and a huge variety of side dishes. They didn't even make it to the dessert table because their plates were too full. Mary Ann led the way to a picnic table that already looked packed, but as they approached everyone shifted to make room for the two of them.

As they started to sit Mary Ann introduced Trey to her friends. She was proud to have the cutie firefighter with her and she knew her crew would be extra nice to him for her sake. They ate and chatted, all her besties telling Trey stories about her. She loved every minute of it.

When they were nearly done eating Terry Anderson cleared his throat. "So, Trey, what do you do in the off season, when you're not fighting fires?"

Before Mary Ann could intervene, Trey swallowed. "I'm a web page designer."

The silence following that statement was deafening, not a sound, not forks on plates, not talking, even the birds stopped singing and the soft breeze quit blowing. Mary Ann groaned internally.

$$\approx$$

TERRY GRINNED. "Are you now? Do you have any business cards in that backpack?" Terry waved his fork toward the backpack behind him.

"Probably, I usually keep some in the little front pocket, that's about all that fits in it."

"Well if you want any peace at all, the rest of today, you'd best be getting them out. Now. Hurry."

Trey reached down to pick up the backpack he'd set on the ground as someone handed it to him. He glanced back to say thanks and saw that he was surrounded by people, with their hands out. He looked over at Terry and then at Mary Ann and raised an eyebrow.

"I told you all about it in the bar the night we had pizza."

He did vaguely remember her talking about web pages, but at the time he'd been in such a state of lust, he hadn't heard a word she'd said. He unzipped the pocket and started handing out his business card, everyone that took one told him they would email him. When he ran out of cards there was still a dozen people waiting for one.

One guy said, "I'll Xerox them."

Another guy shook his head. "I'll email it."

A pretty woman offered, "I'll post it on Facebook."

A kid about twelve, rolled his eyes. "Old people."

The kid took one of the cards scanned it with his phone, tapped the screen and Trey heard hundreds of phones beep with an incoming message. The kid nodded. "Done. Phones, Facebook, Instagram, Pinterest, Newspaper, Twitter and everywhere else."

Trey looked at the kid. "When you get out of high school give me a call."

The kid looked back at his phone and a few taps later, grinned at Trey. "Will do."

Trey's phone beeped, and he looked to see he had a meeting scheduled six years in the future with a person named Keith. He let out a bark of laughter, turned to the kid, and held out his hand. "Nice to meet you, Keith."

The kid grinned at him and shook his hand. Then someone yelled, "Ice cream is ready," and the kid was off like a shot.

Mary Ann giggled. "Ice cream takes precedence."

Trey stood up. "Hell yes, it does. Let's go get some." He pulled Mary Ann to her feet and hustled her to the lines forming. There was a line for vanilla, one for chocolate, and another for strawberry. The vanilla was twice as long as the other two. Trey made a beeline for the vanilla.

Mary Ann said, "What if I want strawberry or chocolate?"

Trey looked at her, clearly torn between being a gentleman and fear he would not get his preferred flavor. He finally sighed and started to step out of line when Mary Ann laughed.

"I didn't say I *did* want chocolate or strawberry, but you get points for being willing. I am totally an old-fashioned girl and want the crème de la crème of homemade ice cream and that, my friend, is vanilla."

He let out a sigh of relief and then frowned at her. "That was mean, you were testing me."

She grinned at him. "Yes, I was. However, I also know they always make about ten times more vanilla than any other flavor."

Trey shook his head. "But *I* didn't know that, and you made me choose."

"I did, and you passed with flying colors, so I will reward you," she stepped closer to him and ran one finger down his chest, "later."

Someone called out, "Mary Ann, you can flirt later, you're holding up the line."

She laughed and stepped forward. Trey decided he might need more than one bowl just to cool down.

After they got their ice cream, Trey remembered what Kristen had said about brownies earlier. "So, Kristen mentioned you brought world famous brownies, today."

"I did, but they are probably all gone by now."

They went over to the dessert table and Mary Ann pointed to the pan that had maybe four crumbs in it and a tiny bit of frosting around the edge of the pan. Trey looked sadly into the pan, he loved brownies, and she even frosted them. He ran his finger around the frosting and then touched the finger to the crumbs. Licking his finger, he hummed his appreciation.

"Delicious, next time save me one."

"I don't know if I can do that, someone would surely notice there was a brownie missing from the pan. You might have to bribe me."

"Oh yeah? What kind of bribe are we talking? A naked one?"

"Yes, that might work nicely, if you bribe me enough I could make you your very own pan."

He stepped closer to her and whispered, "It would be my pleasure, I can think of some things to do with left over frosting."

Her cheeks turned a delightful shade of pink.

Someone said, "Mary Ann your brownie pan is empty, do you have the other one?"

Trey looked at the person speaking, it was Amber, who ran the restaurant in town. He looked back at Mary Ann. "Second one?"

Mary Ann ignored him and reached into the picnic basket under the table and pulled out a full pan of brownies. She put the empty pan back in the basket with what looked to Trey like another full pan. "Here it is."

Amber served herself a brownie and then walked off.

Trey stood in front of the pan so no one else could get to it for a minute and turned towards Mary Ann. "You are so going to get it later, when we get back to your place. Naughty girls must be punished."

Her eyes widened, and she shivered. Trey turned back to the brownie pan and put two of them onto his plate.

While they were eating their ice cream and brownies, which Trey decided were the best he'd ever had, someone spoke over a loud speaker and called everyone's attention.

Trey thought it might be the mayor speaking, but he wasn't positive about that.

"Thanks for coming everyone. We've got a few announcements and then we'll play some games. We'll have two softball games. The annual parents versus kids, and a second one. The hotshot superintendent Grayson Brown has challenged the fire department volunteers to a game." At that statement, Trey's head snapped up and he looked around for the super. None of them had any equipment with them, they were going to be slaughtered. The next words out of the mayor's mouth halted his thoughts in an instant. "And then we'll have the powder puff flag football game, you all know how hard the two teams have been practicing, it should be a great game."

Trey slowly turned his head towards Mary Ann and raised his eyebrows. "Do you play?"

"Of course, I'm on the Water Wenches team and we are going to kick the Brass Nozzles' butt."

Trey thought about watching the ladies in town play football and he could feel a grin slide across his face. "Hot damn, now that is something I have to see." She was a firecracker in bed and on the road, he doubted she was anything but highly competitive in sports. This was going to be something worth remembering. Too bad he didn't have a video camera, he could take some snippets on his phone of course.

She leered at him. "I completely agree, I can't wait to watch you play against the town volunteers. Shirtless."

Trey laughed out loud and then wondered how he was going to play at all, if the woman kept looking at him the way she was.

The mayor spoke over the loudspeaker again. "We'll wrap the whole thing up with the tug of war." She continued, "Now before we get to the games I want all the hotshots from the Fighting Jaguars to come up front. I know there is twenty-one of you and I will be counting, so come on."

Mary Ann pushed at him. "Go on, she won't bite."

Trey reluctantly got to his feet. He didn't want any special attention, he was fairly certain most of the other guys would feel the same. Some would enjoy the limelight, but they were not wild land firefighters for the glory, they were in it to help people. Period. He walked to the front and saw the superintendent Grayson Brown along with the two captains Tyron Jackson and Hideo Mitsuda.

As they approached, Tyron called out, "Form up." So, they split off into their teams with the senior guys in the front row and the rookies in the back row. Three teams of six guys each, plus the three division leaders.

When they were all assembled, the mayor said, "I just wanted everyone to be able to see the men who have been tirelessly working to put out the fires in the mountains, there are some other divisions working on it also, but these are the ones stationed in our area. Fighting Jaguars, we appreciate your hard work on our behalf and want you to know you are always welcome in our town. We hope someday you will be able to come back and enjoy what our town has to offer, rather than spending every minute defending it. Let's give them all a round of applause."

The applause started slowly, but built in force and magnitude until everyone was on their feet clapping and cheering. The sound was deafening and seemed to go on forever. When it started to ebb, the mayor spoke up again. "Hotshots you've just seen a small taste of our gratitude, but that doesn't mean we're not going to try to beat you at softball. May the best team win. Everyone let's head for the games."

The kids game against the parents was a hoot. The police chief pitched for both teams, soft for the kids and as fast as he could throw it for the adults, one of the older kids caught for both teams and Mayor Carol was the umpire. She called the plays in favor of the kids every time. The adults groaned at the injustice, but when it came to them making a play or missing it they looked like a clown team. Missing easy plays and perfect throws, it was hysterical. The kids won the game by two points and were elated.

The Fighting Jaguars lost the softball game, but that wasn't a huge surprise since none of them had played the game in years, and were using borrowed equipment from the town firefighters. Trey hit a triple on one of his at bats, so felt like he had done his part. The score was close, so the Fighting Jaguars were pleased with their performance, even though they lost. Trey did not play shirtless, so Mary Ann whined about that.

The powderpuff football game was nearly vicious, those women were out for blood. Trey enjoyed the heck out of watching Mary Ann and her team fight for every inch of ground. He had never realized she was as determined and competitive as she was, although he supposed he had gotten a taste of it the night she had kissed the stuffing out of him, when that other woman had been coming on to him.

On the field she was a madwoman, talking smack, running like the wind, getting up in the other team's face. It was magnificent to watch, the woman had mad skills and an attitude that didn't quit. Her team managed to squeak ahead of the other team in the last few seconds of the game and she was wild with joy at the win. She and her whole team were gracious winners, changing in an instant from intense rivals to best friends. Trey was surprised as hell at the metamorphosis when the last whistle for the game blew. He was sure there would be fist fights after the competition, but that wasn't the case at all. They all talked about how well the others had done. It was very odd.

CHAPTER 23

When all the competition was finished they returned to the picnic area for drinks, watermelon and whatever desserts were still left. Trey grabbed drinks and plates of watermelon while Mary Ann put out the last pan of her brownies and got them both one with a bit more ice cream. He was going to be stuffed, but he didn't get such treats often, so he had no intention of turning them down. He and Mary Ann sat at a table with Kristen, Nolan, Kyle and Samantha. Chris came over a little while later and wedged in next to Nolan, Chris had a huge mischievous grin on his face and Trey wondered what he was up to. Barbara just shook her head and sat next to her sister.

After they had finished eating Barbara and Kristen started whispering back and forth. Finally, Kristen said, "Fine," and turned to Nolan. "Nolan honey can I see your phone for a minute?'

Nolan handed it over to her without a thought as he continued a discussion with Kyle about which clutch pieces Nolan preferred and the location he wore his in.

Samantha chimed in by asking Nolan if she could see it

and the holster. Nolan unstrapped it from his leg, checked that the safety was on and handed it to Samantha. "This one is lightweight, but still effective for anything I might need it for. Of course, here in Chedwick I probably don't even need to wear it, but it's a habit I don't plan to break."

Chris looked at Kristen as he stood. "Wallet?"

"In the car," Kristen said to Chris and then she looked at Nolan. "Sorry, but it's a rite of passage."

"What do you mean?" Nolan asked as Chris grabbed one arm and Greg grabbed the other and pulled Nolan out of the picnic table. Kyle took one leg and Jeremy took the other.

Nolan started to struggle with the men when the police chief, James MacGregor, appeared by Nolan's side. "Don't fight it, put the cop training on hold, this is all in good fun."

Trey noticed Nolan relax and saw Juan, the other new cop in town, being carried in the same way, with officer Ben trying to talk him down. Juan was putting up a fight, so chief MacGregor hurried over to that group of men.

Trey kept his eyes on the antics but asked Mary Ann, "What's going on?"

Mary Ann laughed. "Just the welcome to our town ritual, be glad you're only here temporarily."

Trey watched in fascination as the men carried the two officers over and dropped them in the stock tanks that had been filled with drinks and watermelon and lots of ice. He'd gotten drinks out of them just a few moments before and the water was ice cold, he shivered at the thought of his whole body being dunked.

Juan swore, and Nolan laughed, as they both climbed out of the tank. Nolan made a beeline for Kristen and gave her a freezing sopping wet hug, then gave Samantha the same treatment. Trey laughed as the women complained that they were only trying to keep his valuables dry.

Several more people were dragged to the stock tanks

including a teenaged girl in very short shorts that had been flirty toward all the younger men. Some people grabbed cups full of the icy water and chased their intended victims with them. Trey laughed at the good clean fun the town people engaged in and was glad he'd been invited to the party. It would be a fun place to live. He looked over at Mary Ann laughing at something one of the women was saying. Yes, a very fun place to live.

MARY ANN WAS HAVING such a great time at the annual picnic, it was fun to be part of a couple at the event she'd gone alone to, for the last several years. Trey seemed to be enjoying himself too. He fit in with her group of friends, like he'd known them all his life. He was such a good sport, even when someone splashed him with the freezing water from the stock tank, he had laughed, shrugged and gone back to talking with Greg.

Samantha sidled up to her. "That's a nice-looking man you have there, girlfriend."

"He is a cutie for sure but he's not really mine. We're just having a fling while he's in town."

Samantha shook her head sadly. "Have you learned nothing, young Padawan. The man is single, owns a business he can do anywhere and is totally hot. Why aren't you going for more than a fling? He's completely into you."

"Do you really think so?" She snuck a peek at him chatting with Greg. He noticed her looking and winked at her.

Samantha laughed. "Well, duh. Of course, he is. Lots of single women in town, don't see him even looking. Even though Theresa has done her best to distract him, the woman is darn near naked and has tried to engage him a couple of times."

Mary Ann bristled. "Theresa better back the hell off, that's my hotshot, well at least until he leaves town. I'm not sharing."

A warm male voice said, "Not sharing what?"

Mary Ann turned and looked at Trey standing slightly behind her. "You, with Theresa."

"Fine by me." He shrugged. "Which one is Theresa?"

Samantha pointed. "That one over there wearing practically nothing."

"Yeah, not interested. I'm already with the prettiest girl here." His eyes widened as his head snapped to Samantha. "Present company excluded... or um included... or... well hell."

Mary Ann felt bad for Trey, he didn't know Samantha was fully secure in herself and was probably getting a kick out of his stammering.

Samantha laughed. "Don't strain anything, dude. You can totally be into Mary Ann without hurting my feelings."

Trey sighed. "Thanks, I didn't mean to offend."

"No offence taken. But next time you come into my bakery, I may give you decaf coffee, instead of the good stuff."

Mary Ann was trying to listen to their conversation with a straight face. Samantha loved to tease. But while Samantha goaded Trey, Mary Ann couldn't help but think about what Samantha had said about Trey being single and able to work from anywhere. Was there a possibility of more? She realized she liked that idea. She liked it a lot.

He grimaced. "Now that's just mean."

Samantha laughed at his wounded expression. "You just take good care of our Mary Ann here and we're square."

Trey put his arm around her waist and drew her close. "My pleasure."

Samantha grinned and wandered off to chat with someone else.

Trey kissed her head and whispered. "So, what's next on the agenda of this picnic?"

Mary Ann put her head on his shoulder as they stood side by side with his arm around her. "While all the wet people change their clothes, they'll bring out the board games. Which they play until it gets too dark to see, and then there will be fireworks over the lake. But we don't have to stay if you want to go back to my place."

"Don't you like the board games and fireworks?"

"Well yes, I do, but I don't want to make you play them. The competition gets a little crazy."

He chuckled. "I'll have you know I'm quite good at board games we played them a lot growing up and still do. We even take wagers on the outcome. As kids it would be chores to swap or pawn off on the loser. As adults it's a little more costly."

She laughed. "With all those sisters I imagine they could cost a bit to appease, if you lost."

He groaned. "You have no idea, we finally had to put a cap on the cost of the prizes."

"So, name your poison, Mahjong, Monopoly, Yahtzee? Those are my favorites, but there are others if you prefer something different."

"Those are fine. Let's go simple, with Yahtzee. I don't want to wear out all my brain cells before I get you home."

She shivered at that. "Oh yeah?"

"Yep, got plans for you, little lady."

"Goody."

As they played games and watched the fireworks, she thought about the fact that he and his family still played board games and realized she couldn't be the one to take him away from his close-knit family. So, while the fantasy of more was fun to think about, the reality was that they were destined for a fling only. And she could admit, if only to herself, that she wished it could be more.

$\mathcal{T}$rey was astonished at the number of emails and phone calls he received over the next two weeks. He changed his voice mail message to tell people who were looking for web development to leave a detailed message, or better yet, send an email describing what they needed. With those instructions in place he could let most of the phone calls go to voice mail. He also put an auto-responder on his email account telling everyone that he would get back to them when he could, but it would probably be after fire season was over. Since most of the emails seemed to be from the town of Chedwick, he figured they would not be anxious to hear from him, while the fire was still filling the valley with smoke.

By the number of emails piling up he was certain he would have work in town for several months, even up to a year. With that information, he started letting himself think about moving to Chedwick. It was a fun town, with plenty of work, but the real reason he was considering it, was because he felt himself falling in love with Mary Ann.

The Fighting Jaguars were back up in the Lucerne-

Holden area continuing to push the fire back from the residents and create a fire break. So, he had plenty of time to think about his relationship with Mary Ann and his future.

Every time he thought about leaving and not seeing her again made his gut clench. Other than the house he owned, there wasn't really any reason to return to his home state, he had friends of course, but all his family had moved away. He felt like he'd already made friends here in the Chelan Valley. So, what was stopping him from making this his permanent home? Well other than he didn't know how Mary Ann would feel about him being around permanently. She mentioned their summer fling often. And lately when she'd said it he didn't like the sound of her putting their relationship in those terms.

He saw Kevin point out the next area they would be tackling. The six of them ringed the area and started the low-level burn, it sure made things easier when the weather was cooperating and today it was. The breeze was gentle, and the days were starting to get cooler so clearly fall was on the way.

As he worked he continued to think about Mary Ann. As far as the amount of actual time they had spent together it was probably less than two weeks but stretched out over several months with a lot of texting and flirting in between actual face time, it felt like they'd been together a lot longer, at least to him. What she was thinking he had no idea, but he thought maybe it was time to talk about it. He would do that as soon as he had the chance.

As the days and nights got colder it became obvious that more rain and maybe even snow was on the horizon, so hopefully they would get relief from the fire soon. Until then they continued to battle the monster and Trey continued to think about Mary Ann.

~

MARY ANN WAS TORN when she heard the forecast for snow in the mountains. On one hand, it would put out the fires and clear the air of the smoke, on the other hand it would send Trey home and out of her life.

She got a text from Trey.

Trey: Snow expected, heading back to Kristen's to wait out the storm. Once it passes we'll go out and see what else needs doing.

Mary Ann: Saw the forecast, will be good to have the fires out.

Trey: Once we are released I want to come into town to see you.

Mary Ann: Of course, you're welcome. I'm sure you have a LOT of people to talk to about web pages and I will be happy to host you while you deal with all of them.

Trey: You've got that right. My phone and email are packed with messages!!! Thanks for letting me stay with you.

Mary Ann: Certainly, I'll take your room and board out in "trade".

Trey: Naked trade?

Mary Ann: That's the best kind!

Trey: No arm twisting required. And we have some things to talk about.

Mary Ann: Sure thing, will be looking forward to it.

Trey: Won't be able to come down until after the snow and cleanup.

Mary Ann: No worries, see you when you get here.

She had no idea what he wanted to talk about, probably just him leaving. But she wasn't going to think about that yet, she would still have a few days with him before he needed to go back to his real life and family.

A lot of people in town had mentioned wanting him to spruce up their web presence, so she hoped he would be able to stay around a week or two getting that all set up. Obviously once he'd talked to everyone about what they wanted he would be able to do the actual work from anywhere. She would be more than happy to keep the man entertained in the evenings.

She hoped it would take him a couple of weeks to tie everything up. She planned to enjoy him for that long. She was certain her heart would be good for a couple of weeks. Any longer than that would be too much for her to bear. She didn't want to get too comfortable having him around. So, a two-week deadline was perfect. That would put their cumulative time together at about a month and anyone, even she, could get over a month-long relationship. Yeah, two weeks would work just fine.

THE FIRE WAS OUT, the cleanup was complete, fire season was officially over. They had cleaned up Kristen's house and the wildlife people had taken the three teen-aged raccoons to reintroduce them to the wild. They were taking the *Cat Boxes* down to Chelan and most of the crew would be heading out on the ferry that afternoon. Trey had volunteered to make sure the transports and all the equipment was put on the barge to ship back to Chelan. Once it was on the barge he was free and clear to do whatever he wanted.

What he planned to do was talk to Mary Ann about staying around and taking their relationship to the next level. He hoped she would be onboard with that idea because he'd already contacted a Realtor to put his house on the market. The Realtor would assess it and inform him on any changes it needed before they listed it. He would need to go back to sign papers and pack up his stuff to drive to Washington, it might take him as long as a month to wrap it all up, providing the house sold. But the guy he'd talked to about selling it had said that baring nothing was wrong, the house would only take a couple of days to find a buyer. The market was hot, and most homes had one open house and enough interest to not need a second one.

Trey's phone rang, it was a Chelan number, not one he recognized, but he was finished with his assignment, so he decided he had time to answer it.

"This is Trey."

"Hi, Trey. This is Jeremy Scott the children's book author, we met at the picnic."

"Sure, I remember, what can I do for you?" he asked.

"Well, I wanted to ask you about any anomalies you saw up in the mountains while you were fighting fires. We've got another guy that's been living off the grid, besides Ted, and I wanted to pick your brain a little. Are you going to stay in town for a little while now that the fires are out?"

Trey laughed. "As a matter of fact, I do plan to stay in town for good. Your town has a lot to offer both in work and a certain female I've grown quite fond of. I haven't talked to Mary Ann about that idea yet, so if you can keep that information on the down low, I would appreciate it."

"You got it. Can I call you in a day or two to talk?"

"Yes, we should be in town later today, so a couple of days would be perfect." He planned to spend the first day with Mary Ann, hopefully in bed. But after that he would have plenty of time during the day for his own activities. So, helping Jeremy would be easy.

He also wanted to look around for a house to buy, that he could put on contingency. He knew Mary Ann's house was a rental, so buying a house would be good, whether he could talk her into being with him or not. He also wanted to see about a store front he could set up his business in. There was probably business license paperwork he would need to get started on. He decided his days would be busy, between all that, and talking to everyone who wanted web pages designed.

"Great I'll call you, and good luck talking to Mary Ann about your idea."

"I hope I won't need it, but I'll take it."

Mary Ann was ready to see Trey. She was going to enjoy their last time together and build up memories to last a lifetime. Then she was going to smile and send him back to his family and friends. There was no way she was going to let on that she longed for more. In fact, she had locked that longing away in a vault and she would not allow it to escape. She was crazy about him, but she wanted him to be happy and tearing him apart from his warm and loving family was a great way to ruin a relationship. Sure, he might be okay with it at first, but eventually he would miss his sisters and parents. Resentment would creep in and it would eventually destroy them both. Nope she wasn't going to let on that she wanted him to stay. Better to have fond memories of a summer fling than end up bitter and hating each other.

She'd thought about tagging along with him but had realized that she didn't really like the idea. This was her town and she loved it. The revelation surprised the heck out of her, because for years she'd thought of nothing except getting out of Chedwick and exploring the world. And while traveling still did appeal to her, she wanted to come back to her little town when her vacation ended. She loved the art gallery work and creating jewelry with Kristen. She was happy in this place and if the price for that happiness was a relationship with Trey, well she had reluctantly decided the price was worth it.

With that decision she was eager to see him and enjoy the

last few days. She'd ordered a few things to spice up their time together. Online adult toy stores had lots of fun things to try. She planned to send him away exhausted with plenty of memories of their time together. Starting with the sexy lingerie she had on under her sedate clothing. The contrast helped her feel sexy.

CHAPTER 25

The Fighting Jaguars' made it to town a couple hours before the ferry would arrive. They stowed the *Cat boxes* at the dock for the barge. It would come in the day after tomorrow and they'd already paid for passage. Trey would meet the barge and make sure their transport vehicles got loaded on.

They all walked over to Greg's to have a beer and some food while they waited for the ferry to take them to Chelan.

Greg grinned when they walked into his place. It sure looked different during the day, with all the light coming in the windows from what Trey thought of as *the game room*. Plus, all the house lights were on full.

Greg came over to them. "Hotshots, welcome to my abode. I assume you're on your way out of town, now that the fire has been tamed."

Kevin nodded. "Yep, we are waiting for the ferry to take us back to our homes, it's been a long fire season. All except Trey here, he seems to have gotten his foot caught in the door of your little town."

Brandon laughed. "Not sure that's the right part of his anatomy that is caught, but you get the drift."

Trey elbowed his buddy. "Knock it off, Brandon."

The guys just laughed at his reticence to talk about his honey and started ordering food and drinks. Trey knew they didn't mean anything by it, but it seemed kind of low class to talk about Mary Ann that way.

They ate and drank and when the ferry horn sounded its arrival they paid their tab and hustled out to be on their way home. Trey fist bumped his friends and wasn't the least bit inclined to get on the ferry.

Once the boat was on its way he went by the flower shop to get Mary Ann some flowers. He was glad it was open. She seemed to like flowers, she'd gushed about the bouquet they had sent for the gallery's opening day. And he didn't want to buy her jewelry again, since he wasn't quite sure that hadn't been a bit of a disaster. She'd said she wanted to keep the earrings, but he still felt there was something a little off about that gift.

As he walked down the street, with his purchase, toward the art gallery he noticed a store front right on the corner that was available for lease. He took a picture of the sign with his phone and decided to call Kyle Moore in a few days to ask about it. He was pretty sure this Kyle was one of Mary Ann's group and he'd met him at the fire department and at the picnic. He didn't really know anyone's last name, so it could be someone different. But with only a thousand residents how many Kyle's could there be? Since he was a Realtor he could probably ask him about any houses that were for sale too. Happy that things seemed to be going his way he strolled on.

～

MARY ANN SQUIRMED in her chair as she worked on the books. The sexy underwear was driving her crazy. She'd thought it would be fun to wear it to work while she waited for Trey, but she had been wrong about that idea. It had caused her to think about having sex with the man. All. Day. Long. That was a long time, a very long time, for those kinds of ideas to be floating through her brain. She'd tried to keep the thoughts out with work, but it had not helped. Even though she loved her job, her body had been on fire the entire day.

Thank God, she'd arranged to take the day off tomorrow, because she was certain she was going to bang that man for the next twenty-four hours straight.

When he finally walked in the door she didn't know whether to cry or cheer. She just sat and watched him walk in with his easy grace and killer looks. He was dressed in jeans and a T-shirt with the wildland firefighter Maltese cross on the pec, a large backpack sat on his shoulders and hugged his body and he was carrying a bouquet of flowers.

He saw her and started ambling her direction. She walked around her work table and met him, walking straight into his arms. She grabbed his hair and pulled his head down to hers for a fiery kiss.

She heard someone come in from the back room but didn't let go until Tim said, "Woah. You guys are going to start a fire in here with all that heat."

Mary Ann turned her head to see the young man standing there, beet red, trying not to gawk. "Well now that you're here, Tim, I'll let you take over, and I'll take this firefighter home to see what kind of conflagration we can stir up."

Tim nodded. "I hope you won't have to call the fire department to put out the flames."

Trey laughed. "Me too, Tim, me too."

Mary Ann snatched up her purse, waved goodbye and took her man with her out the door.

As they walked to her orange rocket Trey didn't say another word. When he got to the door, he shook his head and looked at her. "That was some greeting. I brought you flowers but we might have incinerated them."

She laughed. "I think they'll be fine. Thank you, they are lovely."

"Did you even look at them?"

She laughed again and looked him up and down. "Nope, too busy ogling you."

"Well okay then, let's get to your house before something happens right here in the street."

He stowed all his gear in the back of her car and climbed in. She saw him clutch onto the chicken bar. Then he looked at her. "Drive fast."

She laughed and pealed out of the parking lot. Fortunately, she made it home without any of Chedwick's finest catching her speeding again.

She unlocked the door and Trey followed her in. He kicked the door closed and she heard the lock snick shut. Dropping his back pack and her flowers to the floor, he pulled her into him, fisted his hands in her hair and kissed her with an intensity that startled her.

"Whoa, what got into you?"

He shrugged. "I was fine until you kissed the breath out of me in the gallery. In fact, I had planned to look around a bit while you closed up shop. But you kissed me, and all the blood drained out of my head and I couldn't remember my name, let alone what I had planned to do. Now my question is what got you so riled up?"

"Rather than tell you I'll show you." She unbuttoned the top few buttons on the pretty Polka-dot dress she had on and let it float down her body. She was gratified by his eyes going wide and almost instantly opaque.

He swallowed. "Did you wear those scraps of lace all day?"

She nodded and ran her fingers across the lace barely covering her breasts.

"Well no wonder you were so enthusiastic in your greeting, you look amazing." He reached out and covered one breast with his hand and ran his thumb over the already hard nipple. "Beautiful."

"Thanks, they about drove me crazy all day reminding me you were on your way to see me. I took tomorrow off so we can spend it together. But I'll have to work the rest of the week."

"Good, I was hoping we could spend tomorrow together. And after that I have a ton of people to meet with to talk about web pages. But I don't want to think about that right now, because there isn't enough blood left in the upper half of my body. I just want to enjoy you and those scraps of lace."

He scooped her up to carry her to her bedroom. "Excellent plan, Trey."

CHAPTER 26

They spent the next thirty-six hours in a lust filled haze. Trey was amused by the sex toys she'd purchased online and did his best to fulfill her every fantasy. But he could admit, if only to himself, that the woman had worn him out. She was like the damn Energizer bunny. Constantly. Moving.

The second morning she had bounded out of bed slapped him on the ass and told him she was off to work.

He'd tried to rouse himself, unsuccessfully.

She'd just laughed and kissed him on the cheek as she raced out the door. He thought he might stay right there in bed for the next eight or nine hours to build enough stamina for the evening to come.

But that was not meant to be, as phone calls started coming in. He heard from Jeremy and a few other towns people and started setting up meetings. He called Kyle and it was the same guy he'd met earlier, so he set up a time to get together with him later in the week.

The first thing he did was meet with Jeremy and Hank Jefferson to talk about the other guy that was living off the grid. Jeremy picked him up from Mary Ann's to drive him out to the ranch.

"Hey, Trey. Thanks for taking some time for this." Jeremy said, as Trey climbed into the jeep.

"No problem. This is my new home town, so I need to be a part of it—and if that means looking for a guy down on his luck, I'm there."

"New home town? So, you and Mary Ann are…"

Trey wasn't sure exactly what to say. He hadn't been able to talk to Mary Ann about his plans to stay, but he certainly hoped when he did she would be on board. "I plan to marry that woman. As soon as I can convince her of that idea. So, yes. This is my permanent home town. I'll have to go back and pack up my house and move all my crap here, but that should only take a few weeks. And I'll still have to go other places during fire season, but the rest of the year, I'm here."

Trey spoke boldly and with confidence he didn't really feel. He hoped he didn't end up looking like an idiot.

They chatted about web pages as they drove onto the ranch and parked by the house.

While Jeremy unpacked a backpack of all kinds of supplies Hank filled him in on the person they were looking for. It was a guy Hank's age who was out of the military and homeless. That pissed Trey off because he didn't think it was right that a man should serve his country, and then end up homeless.

He took the big map Jeremy had covered with a plastic sleeve and a felt tip pen.

"I was thinking I could start by outlining where the fire was on the big map and I can mark places where we found odd things." He'd studied the maps they had used at their base of operations often enough he was certain he could draw them on the copies Jeremy had brought.

"Sounds like a plan," Hank chimed in.

While Trey started marking the big map, Jeremy and Hank took the more detailed ones and added in the things they knew about. They were going by the guy's personality and upbringing; which Trey thought was a clever idea.

When they all finished they circled the locations that seemed the most likely and decided to search those areas in the mornings. That way they could do their regular work in the afternoons. Trey was happy to join the search party, so he started scheduling all his meetings after lunch.

Now if he could just get Mary Ann to talk about the future. Every time he tried to bring it up she shut him down and refused. Saying she didn't want to change their status, that she was happy enjoying their summer fling.

His oldest sister called him one afternoon while he was thinking about Mary Ann and her reticence to talk about the future.

"Hey Gabs, howzit?"

"Trey, you know I hate that name."

"Of course, I do. That's why I use it. It's the brother's duty to torment."

She sighed, and he grinned. Mission accomplished.

"I *called* to find out about this move you're making. Why on earth are you moving to some Podunk town in eastern Washington none of us have ever heard of?"

"It's a very nice little town in the Chelan valley."

"Yes. I know. I looked it up, there are no roads to it. Except for a forest service road that shows it as unpaved, most of the way. The website, which by the way, needs a ton of work, said you must take a ferry to get to it. Or in the summer there is a seaplane, that's like six seats. I repeat why in the hell? If you want to move why aren't you moving closer to one of us?"

He didn't know how to get out of this conversation, so he

hedged. "Well, let's see, part of the answer you noticed your-self, the website needs work."

"Which you could do perfectly well from anywhere."

"The town is really warm and friendly, and everyone is begging me to do their web pages."

"I repeat, which you could—"

Fine he would just spill it. "And I met a woman."

She squealed. "What? You met a woman? While on hotshot location? But you never get involved with locals."

"This one is a force of nature. I had no choice. And I'm crazy about her."

"So, are you like, getting married?"

Shit. He wasn't ready to go there, but maybe his sister could give him some hints. "We haven't really talked about that, but that's my plan."

"And her plan?"

"She says she's happy with it being a summer fling."

"You're selling your house, moving to another state, to some little remote town, for a woman who is a summer fling?" Each word she said got louder until she was shouting in his ear.

"No. I love her. I just haven't managed to pin her down long enough to talk about making it permanent. Her actions don't really match what comes out of her mouth. One minute she is clinging to me like she will never let go, the next she laughs, pushes me away and talks about us being a summer fling. It's almost like she's reading a script and the smile that goes with the words doesn't reach her eyes. I have to admit I'm confused. Any insights, sister dear?"

"She does sound conflicted. Is she a summer fling type of person, never happy with one guy? Have you asked any of the locals?"

"No, but that's not a bad idea. Although it seems a little stalkerish to me."

"Not really. If you grew up there you would know, wouldn't you?"

He thought of how everyone in the town knew everything and had to agree. "Yes, I would. I'll see about asking. I'm meeting with half the town in the next few days to talk about web pages."

"Try to pick someone discreet. But I think you need to find out about this before you move, don't you? What if she doesn't truly want a relationship? Then you'll have moved for nothing."

"Maybe. I'll think about it. So, what's happening in your life?"

They chatted for a few more minutes and he told her he would keep in touch now that fire season was over.

After the call he thought about what she'd said. What if Mary Ann really didn't want a relationship? Did he want to move here if not? Was he only moving to be with her? What if it didn't work out between them? Would he still be happy with the move? He thought about it long and hard and decided that yes, he really did want to live here. There was a ton of work and he liked the way the town had welcomed him.

He'd never lived in such a small town before. It had freaked him out some at first, but he'd learned to enjoy it. They were a caring community and he found himself wanting to be a part of it. As he talked with people to set up appointments and determine web needs, he'd gotten a sense of what they were trying to do, and he wanted to be a part of helping the little town flourish.

He was still going to try his best to get Mary Ann on board for a permanent relationship, but since he decided he wasn't going anywhere it wasn't an urgent need. He could work on her over the next six months, before the start of next year's fire season. If he hadn't convinced her by then, well they had years to go. But he might think about talking to one of the guys about Mary Ann's former relationships.

~

MARY ANN WAS AN EMOTIONAL MESS. She was trying so hard to stay in the moment and enjoy Trey for the last few weeks. But her heart was begging her to change her mind. He kept bringing up the topic and it scared the hell out of her so much, that she shut him down with a laugh and bullshit words about enjoying the fling.

The pretense was killing her, and she wasn't sure she could keep it up much longer. She was starting to wish he would just go already, so she could move on with her life. But then she would think about that and panic and hold him tight, so he couldn't leave. A long-distance relationship was not appealing and him staying here was not in the cards. There was no way that she would be the reason he moved away from his family.

At least he was busy during the day, so she could work. In the mornings he was helping track some old guy who had caused the fire in Amber's back room. Apparently, the guy was homeless, and Amber had been letting him stay in the banquet room at night, since the forest fire had forced him to evacuate his campground in the mountains. She hoped they could find him.

In the afternoons he was gathering all the information about what everyone in town wanted done with their websites. She wasn't sure he would be able to get to all of them before he left. But she thought a lot of it could probably be done over the phone or email.

She sighed as she worked on a pendant Kristen had given her. One of Kristen's long-term clients had bought a malachite cabochon and wanted a simple setting. It was Mary

Ann's first attempt working with a stone. Kristen was very particular about the bezel setting that would hold the cab and had already rejected Mary Ann's first two attempts, telling her that the setting would make or break the piece, especially since it was such a simple design.

Kristen looked up. "Are you having trouble?"

Mary Ann frowned, confused by the question. "With the setting? No, actually I think this one might finally work."

"Then why the sigh?"

Mary Ann waved her hand but felt tears threaten. She looked back down at what she was doing.

Kristen turned off her torch and rolled her chair over to Mary Ann. "I'm not the most observant person on the planet, but even I can tell something is wrong. Now spill."

Mary Ann looked up and smiled at Kristen, but she wasn't sure she pulled it off, when Kristen flinched.

"It's nothing important." Kristen just sat there blinking at her. "I'm being silly. I never planned on anything long term. It's a summer fling. It started that way and it's going to end that way."

Kristen nodded. "Ah, the cutie firefighter."

Mary Ann sighed again. "Yeah. I'll be sad to see him go."

"Of course, you will, he's been a lot of fun and is a nice guy. No reason to not be a little down about his leaving. It's normal."

Mary Ann shrugged. "But I've known all along. It's not a surprise, or anything."

"No, but it's still a loss, even if it is an expected one. You could probably keep in touch."

"No way. I have no interest in a long-distance relationship." Mary Ann was certain she would not like that at all.

"In that case enjoy him until he leaves. Kiss him goodbye. Then take the day off to cry and eat ice cream. Two days even. Then dust yourself off and move on."

Mary Ann smiled. "That sounds like great advice. I'll try it."

"Good." Kristen looked down at the bezel Mary Ann had almost finished. "You're right, that does look good. I think you've got this one."

Mary Ann smiled and decided that while she was losing the guy she still had a pretty sweet life.

CHAPTER 27

A week and a half after Trey had been turned loose from the fire, his Realtor called him and told him he needed to get back there as soon as possible. They'd had an inspection done and had looked through his house and felt certain they could get it sold immediately, but he needed to get back there to clean it out. The guy said they needed most of his crap packed up and a lot of his furniture removed. It seemed like they wanted a very empty look, to show to potential buyers.

He thought about speeding up the timing of his move and decided he liked that idea, they had found Owen, the homeless vet, and Hank was going to give him a home and a job if he wanted one. There were no other commitments he couldn't move, so he told them he would be back by the end of the week. The ferry had already come by earlier, so he could go tomorrow. That would give him one more day to talk to Mary Ann.

He made ferry and flight reservations for the trip and started gathering his belongings to put in his backpack.

Mary Ann walked into her room and found him packing. She froze in the doorway. "Oh hi, are you leaving?"

He tried to gauge her reaction but could get no sense of it. Either she didn't care, or she was better at hiding her emotions than he would have guessed. He turned and walked over to her, taking her hands. "Yeah, I need to get back and sign some paperwork, but I'll be back—"

She pulled one hand free and put it over his mouth stilling his words. "Don't make promises you aren't going to be able to keep. I've had a great time with you Trey, but this needs to be goodbye. I'm not interested in a long-term relationship. We knew this fling had an expiration date and I'm good with that. You've got a life somewhere else and I'm happy here. So, let's just make wild passionate love one last time tonight and move on. Okay?"

Fuck that, he was tired of her avoiding any discussion of the future. He was going to talk to her if he had to hog tie her.

But before he could say a word, her face turned to stone and she crossed her arms. "If that's not okay with you, then I'll just say good bye now and go stay with a friend tonight. I don't want anything more Trey, this is it."

He didn't know whether to argue or walk out himself. But he wasn't a fool and he wanted one last night with her. If she really meant what she said, that she didn't want a long-term relationship, he didn't want to miss this last opportunity to love her with his body. But he hoped like hell he could convince her when he came back in a few weeks. "Fine."

She smiled like she didn't quite believe him, which was wise because he didn't quite believe him either.

The next afternoon Trey was in a crappy mood when he boarded the ferry. He'd woken to an empty house. Mary Ann had left him a note saying she was happy to have known him and she wished him a good life. What the fuck, she couldn't even say goodbye? Her phone went straight to voicemail when he called, like it was turned off.

Going to the gallery did him no good, some woman he'd never seen before told him she'd called in sick. He'd walked through town looking for her car but couldn't find it anywhere. It wasn't at Greg's bar or Samantha's bakery or Amber's restaurant, or any of the streets he walked up and down on. They had never gone anywhere except to eat, so he didn't really know where else to look for her.

He finally gave up and spent the rest of the morning calling to cancel the appointments he had scheduled with the town people. Promising them he would reschedule in a few weeks. He didn't go into any details with them, just said he was going to be leaving quickly, but wouldn't forget about their needs.

He was not happy with how he'd left it with Mary Ann, she was a determined woman and had not allowed him to talk about returning. Well she'd be damn surprised when he showed back up in a few weeks with a trailer full of his stuff. It's not the way he'd hoped it would go, but he could handle it and if she really did mean she didn't want a relationship with him, well he'd just have to live with that.

As he rode the ferry down to Chelan he made a list of all he needed to accomplish while he was gone. He'd already turned in paperwork to get a Washington business license, but there were a lot of things to do to wrap up his old life before he made the move.

~

MARY ANN SAT high on the mountain and watched as the ferry took the best man she'd ever known away. She'd left her house before the sun was up and had been sitting up here the entire day. Trey would be pissed at her disappearance, but maybe that was a good thing. It might help him get over her faster.

She knew she was a coward to run out on him this morning, but she couldn't stand the idea of saying goodbye and she knew he would try to talk to her about a long-term relationship. But this last ten days had been brutal. With the deadline of his leaving looming over her, she'd been a wreck. Better to have it finally over. A clean break rather than stringing it along. Trying to make a long-distance relationship work sucked and would end up with more heartbreak when the string finally snapped. Better to get it over with quickly and cleanly, so that she could start the healing process.

She was determined. Their last night together had been both wonderful and devastating. Trey had made love to her over and over, with a thoroughness that bordered on obsession or maybe desperation. She'd felt the same way, like she was trying to memorize his body. Every touch, every taste was a frantic attempt to save the memory for the future, when their lives went separate directions and all they had left was memories.

So, while the love making was exquisite the motivation behind it turned it bitter and heartbreaking. She watched the ferry disappear while her maudlin thoughts circled, and her tears flowed. After it was gone she continue to stare at where it had been. She had no idea how long she sat there, but she finally roused herself. It was time to drive down the mountain to her home. She wondered if she could stand to live there now with memories of Trey in every room. Or if she should consider moving. Maybe it was time to buy something.

Mary Ann gave herself two days to grieve, as Kristen had suggested, and then she dragged herself back to work. But her enthusiasm was sorely lacking. She still enjoyed designing jewelry, but she didn't feel very creative, so she was glad when Kristen gave her things she'd already done before.

The gallery continued to have plenty of customers and sales. Now that the fire was out on the mountain and the smoke had cleared, a lot of people said they had been biding their time until they could come in, without any health concerns.

A whole group of senior citizens came in one day.

"We finally felt safe to come see this new art gallery," one older gentleman said.

"Yes. The smoke made us nervous. We live in Wenatchee," a sprightly woman piped up.

"We've had the tour bus people on hold for months. We called them every day to let them know that it wouldn't be today. Until it was!" a woman leaning on her cane said with a sparkle in her eye.

Mary Ann wondered who had been more excited that the air was finally clear enough, the seniors or the tour bus company.

They looked through every single item in the store and each person selected one thing to purchase. Some were very small and very inexpensive, others were higher priced. When the final total was added up, after the group had gone back to the ferry landing, Mary Ann realized that it had been an excellent sales day.

A few days later Lucille sent more of her glass art, and Kristen actually let Mary Ann open it, without Nolan or anyone else there, to monitor the unpacking. They were so beautiful, but even they, did not vanquish her lethargy.

She thought about calling or texting Trey, just to say hi,

but she chickened out. The day he left she had blocked his number and she hadn't changed that. Some day when she was feeling stronger she would unblock it and send him a friendly text, apologizing for not seeing him off. But she wasn't there yet, so she left it as is.

CHAPTER 28

*M*ary Ann decided she had missed seeing Samantha, so she roused herself enough to go into the bakery. She wasn't really hungry, but maybe the bakery would inspire her to eat something.

"Well it's about time you came in. I haven't seen you forever," Samantha said, when she came out of the back room after the door chimed.

"Yeah, I know. Sorry about that. I've been in kind of a funk since Trey left. I kept telling myself I was happy with our relationship being a summer fling. But the idea of never seeing him again has kind of knocked the wind out of my sales."

Samantha shook her head. "That's the silliest thing you've ever said, Mary Ann Thompson. Trey *is* coming back to town. He bought the blue house in Chris and Barbara's neighborhood last week.

Mary Ann snapped her gaze to Samantha. She didn't believe it.

Samantha continued, "Kyle was telling me all about it last night. In fact, Kyle told me Trey looked at it before he left town and put in an offer on the spot, contingent on the sale of his other house. That house sold last Monday, so Kyle's been busy getting everything in order, so Trey can move in as soon as all his stuff gets here."

Mary Ann shook her head in denial. "But he has another life and his family…."

"Well I don't know about that, but Kyle said he also leased the storefront over on Anderson avenue—that's been vacant —to set up his internet design business. He told Kyle he wanted to be able to meet with clients and wanted a shop, rather than working out of his home like he's been doing."

Mary Ann shook her head still not able to believe it. "I had no idea. Why would he do that?"

Samantha laughed. "Maybe it has something to do with a sexy art gallery curator. A *clueless* sexy curator, that is."

"But I told him I wasn't interested in a long-term relationship."

"Did you now, so why have you been sulking and depressed the three weeks he's been gone?"

"I haven't been depressed and sulking." *Much.*

"Oh yeah." Samantha took her by the arm, marched her into the bathroom, flipped on the light, and shoved her in front of a mirror. "Then explain to me why you look like crap."

Mary Ann looked at herself in the mirror and winced. Okay so maybe she had been a little sad, and maybe she hadn't been as fastidious about her appearance as she normally was, and she could admit she hadn't had much of an appetite, but shedding a few pounds never hurt anyone.

Samantha didn't let her answer, instead she drug her to the door and pushed her through it. "Now go clean up and eat something."

Mary Ann decided she could go home and shower and do some laundry and maybe eat a sandwich. But only because her friend was forcing her to. Not because she might see Trey again, nope for Samantha. Although she might put on her black sundress with the flowers printed on it and her knee-high boots, that particular outfit always gave her confidence. She might need it.

～

TREY KNOCKED on Mary Ann's door, determined to convince this woman to give him a chance. He'd missed her like crazy the three weeks he'd been gone. He'd driven off the barge pulling the trailer with all his worldly possessions, unhooked it, leaving it in the driveway of his new house and come straight here to Mary Ann's home.

Mary Ann opened the door. "Trey what are you doing here?"

He ignored her question, drinking her in with his eyes, it was like looking at the sun after a long cold, cloudy winter. "I'm staying, you know."

She turned her back on him and walked onto her house, leaving the door open for him to follow. He went inside and closed the door. She whirled around waving her hands in the air. "Yeah, I kind of gathered that when you bought the house and opened a business. Won't your family miss you?"

He shrugged. "No. We'll still facetime and get together a couple of times a year like we've always done."

She cocked her head to the side. "What do you mean get together a couple times a year. I thought you got together all the time."

"No, that's kind of hard to do when we're spread across the country. We facetime every week, come hell or high water, unless I'm on a fire. Then they just do it without me."

Mary Ann frowned at him like she was trying to decipher his words. "You don't all live in the same city?"

"No. Whatever gave you that idea?"

"I thought you did, talking about all the things you did together. Like playing board games."

"Online board games, Mary Ann. We play them online."

She slumped into a chair that was close by. "Well, hell. You mean I sent you away to be with your family and thought I would never see you again and you don't even live in the same town?"

"Ah, so that's why you did it."

"Yes, I was being all self-sacrificing for you, and depriving myself. And you don't even live in the same town? I went through all that heartbreak for nothing?" Each word she said got shriller until she was nearly screeching.

A slow smile slid over Trey's features. "Heart break? Really?"

She nodded woodenly.

"Cool."

Mary Ann frowned. "Why is that cool?"

"I've been wracking my brain trying to figure out how to get from summer fling status to a real boyfriend, or even a fiancé."

Her eyes widened. "Fiancé?"

"Yes, Mary Ann. I am head over heels in love with you, and I want you to marry me."

"Oh. I had no idea."

He took her hands and pulled her up out of the chair and into his arms. "Obviously. So, what do you think of the idea? Any chances of you making me the happiest guy in town?"

"Well I suppose I might be persuaded to consider moving you from summer fling to boyfriend status."

He moved in closer pulling her to him. "And…"

She giggled and tipped her face up to his. "And maybe fiancé status, since I love you, too."

Trey picked her up by the waist and twirled her around.

She hung on tight and laughed. "Let's go celebrate with some of that summer fling action."

"You got it, my little wildcat."

～

THE NEXT MORNING Mary Ann kissed Trey goodbye. He needed to get to work, he had a meeting with Terry about the website he wanted him to build for his custom furniture business. Mary Ann had a couple of hours before she needed to be at the art gallery. She would normally go in early to work on jewelry, but this morning she wanted to sit and revel in the fact that Trey was back and wanted to marry her.

She decided to indulge in another cup of coffee when Trey walked back in with a very odd expression on his face. "What is it?"

"Come see." He took her hand and led her out to the street. There in front of her house was his car, and it was filled with soda cans and then cling wrapped, with so much cling wrap you could hardly tell what color it was. But the most surprising thing, was the town peacock standing on top of the car with his feathers in full array.

Mary Ann laughed. "Looks like you've been given the stamp of approval by the firefighters and the peacock. Welcome to Chedwick, Trey."

The End

Dear Reader,

I love firefighters. My dad was a volunteer firefighter in my home town of Wheat Ridge Colorado. We lived four houses down from the fire station and for a while the ambulance sat in our driveway. So we always had firefighters in the house. My parents were young and social, so they had an open-door policy and loved to have friends stop by.

When I decided to write the Lake Chelan series, I wanted to put in a volunteer fire department like the one down the street. As kids we spent a lot of time in the fire department and walking into one now, still smells like home to me.

And if I see firefighters out on the corners collecting money for charity with their boots, I can't drive by without throwing a couple of dollars in. With a catch in my throat and a tear in my eye.

So when it came to writing the Lake Chelan books I put in a fire department like the one from my childhood. Nearly all the Lake Chelan books have a firefighter in the starring role or as a strong secondary character. You'll find fun and pranks galore. Just exactly the way I grew up.

My parents were young and the pranks we all pulled on each other... well you'll just have to read the books. Some are true pranks from my teenage years and some are straight out of my imagination. It's up to you to determine which are which.

Shirley Penick

ABOUT THE AUTHOR

What does a geeky math nerd know about writing romance?

That's a darn good question. As a former techy I've done everything from computer programming to international trainer. Prior to college I had lots of different jobs and activities that were so diverse, I was an anomaly.

None of that qualifies me for writing novels. But I have some darn good stories to tell and a lot of imagination.

I have lived in Colorado, Hawaii and currently Washington. Going from two states with 340 days of sun to a state with 340 days of clouds, I had to do something to perk me up. And that's when I started this new adventure called author. Joining the Romance Writers of America and two local chapters, helped me learn the craft quickly and has been a ton of fun.

My family consists of two grown children, their spouses, two adorable grand-daughters, and one grand dog. My favorite activity is playing with my grand-daughters!

When the girls can't play with their amazing grandmother, my interests are reading and writing, yay! I started reading at a young age with the Nancy Drew mysteries and have continued to be an avid reader my whole life. My favorite reading material is romance in most of the genres, but occasionally other stories creep into my to-be-read pile, I don't kick them out.

Some of the strange jobs I have held are a carnation grower's worker, a trap club puller, a pizza hut waitress, a software engineer, an international trainer, and a business program manager. I took welding, drafting and upholstery in high school, a long time ago when girls didn't take those classes, so I have an eclectic bunch of knowledge and experience.

And for something really unusual… I once had a raccoon as a pet.

Join with me as I tell my stories, weaving real tidbits from my life in with imaginary ones. You'll have to guess which is which. It will be a hoot.

∾

Contact me:
www.shirleypenick.com
www.facebook.com/ShirleyPenickAuthor

To sign up for Shirley's New Release Newsletter, send email to shirleypenick@outlook.com, subject newsletter.